Lady Isla and the Lord of Rogues

Merry Spinsters, Charming Rogues

Sofi Laporte

http://www.sofilaporte.com

GPSR compliance:
Alice Lapuerta
c/o Block Services
Stuttgarter Str. 106
70736 Fellbach, Germany
sofi@sofilaporte.com

Editor: Rebecca Paulinyi
Cover Art: Victoria Cooper

Chapter One

LADY ISLA ROTHVALE, a proper and respectable spinster, had accomplished the unthinkable: she'd accidentally killed a man with her umbrella.

She wouldn't have thought it possible, given that her umbrella was an old and tattered thing with a blunt tip. But when the man had lunged out of a dark alley with a snarl, it seemed the most reasonable course of action to jab its tip into his stomach to keep him at bay. To her utter astonishment, he staggered back, stumbled over a stone step, and collapsed to the ground.

Dead.

There wasn't a more gentle or peace-loving person in all of London than Lady Isla. She was a respectable and well-liked member of the *ton*, meticulously running her brother's household, visiting orphanages, hospitals, and prisons, making morning calls with prominent members of society, and attending their balls and galas in the evenings. Her sweet-tempered and cheerful nature abhorred violence. Thus, it was a considerable surprise to her when she wielded her umbrella without hesitation or the tiniest whisper of conscience and saw with immense satisfaction that its mark had been true.

Reverend Whitlow, esteemed leader of her parish, would be horrified, was the first thought that shot through her befuddled mind. But this wasn't the moment to think about what Reverend Whitlow would have thought. She should have been scandalised by her own behaviour, but the strange thing was that she wasn't. Not in the least.

After all, the man had threatened to *kiss her.*

And heaven knew what other deeds, too horrible to contemplate.

The wretch had jumped out of the shadows, and, when she'd offered him her purse, which held several coins, he'd laughed.

"There's something else I want," he'd said in a tone that made her shudder. "Something infinitely more delicious."

"And what would that be?" Lady Isla had enquired. A mistake, as she now knew, for one ought to never negotiate with criminals.

"A kiss from those rosy-red lips of yours," he'd said with a leer and stepped towards her.

His intention was plain: he intended to violate them, and that couldn't be. She cherished her life, and she was responsible for Meggie's, too. She'd vowed to protect her maid when she'd wheedled her into accompanying her to St Giles Rookery, London's most dangerous slum.

So, when the man lunged at her, she wielded her umbrella like a rapier and hit her target.

The man fell.

The umbrella dropped to the ground with a clatter.

Meggie bent close to his face. "No breath, m'lady. Lawks. Now you went and did 'im in."

Isla bent over the man. There was blood oozing over the cobbled stones, though it wasn't wholly clear whether that came from the hole in his stomach or from the edge of the step where he'd cracked his head as he stumbled backwards.

Either way, it didn't matter, did it?

She gently nudged him with her booted foot. He didn't move. "Oh dear," she breathed. "He appears quite dead."

"Yer brother won't be pleased," Meggie prophesied.

Not to mention the scandal when they hanged her in Newgate for murder.

What now?

"I suppose we must take him along," she said after a moment's hesitation.

"'E's dead as mutton, m'lady. Why take a corpse along? The evidence of murder." Meggie asked. "They'll find it, have ye clapped into Newgate and hang ye."

Hearing these fearful thoughts voiced so immediately after she herself had thought them, in those very words too, was uncommonly distressing.

Isla swallowed.

"I knows exactly what to do in situations like these," Meggie went on. "Trust me, m'lady, I've had my share of experience in this."

Isla did not doubt it, for Meggie was one of her rescue projects she had picked up from the rookery.

She was now her maid, and she'd been faithful and a good citizen ever since. But her past experience could come in handy now she found herself in such circumstances.

She therefore asked, "Tell me then, in your extensive experience of dealing with such matters—what does one do?"

"Take yer skirts in yer hands and run."

It was a sound idea and very tempting. Her fingers cramped around the material of her skirts. She took one step, two steps away, then froze.

Isla scrunched her nose together, something she did every time she thought deeply.

"No. That makes us appear guilty. But it was self-defence," she heard her voice say. "*In self-defence, the person attacked must do all he can to avoid the necessity of his defence; he must retreat as far as he can with safety, and then if a man pursues him with intent to murder, he may kill him in his own defence.*" She cleared her throat. "From Sir Michael Foster's *Crown Law.*" Algie had the book lying about in his study and when she was especially bored in her free time, she tended to read a little of it. Just for amusement.

"So, Meggie," she continued, her frown clearing, "the following questions must be asked: did he pursue us with the intent to murder?"

Meggie tilted her head thoughtfully. "'E clearly wanted a kiss. But murder? All and sundry knows a body enters St Giles alive but leaves as a corpse, so—aye, that's exactly what 'e would've done. It was good ye did 'im in before 'e did ye in." Meggie sniffed. "Otherwise, it'd be you lyin' there." She thought and then added. "And me atop."

"So, we may reasonably conclude that he threatened us, and I had a right to kill him?"

Meggie thought for a moment. " 'E didn't actually take the purse when ye offered it, did 'e? Scared us out of our bleedin' skin by stepping out of the shadow like that. And 'e made a grab for yer arm. Saw it with my own eyes. No doubt 'is intention was to murder and kidnap and ravish and rob ye." Meggie seemed to take a clear delight in listing all the horrible deeds he could have committed. "Aye. 'Twas good to kill 'im there and then."

Isla swallowed. "The order of things may be nego-tiable, but he was an evident threat. So, you see, Meggie, it was self-defence. With some luck, I shall not be confined in Newgate and hanged after all." She heaved a sigh of relief.

The two women looked down at the body. Isla bent over him. The last rays of sunlight did not reach the floor of the narrow, greasy alley. She squinted. In the semi-shadow, she saw the head of a red wolf printed on the wooden door, behind the body.

Meggie prodded the body with her foot. "Dead," she declared, as if that hadn't already been established. "And if 'e ain't yet, 'e'll soon be."

"The last thing we can do for him is give him a decent burial," Isla decided. "Call John to help us take him along."

John was their footman.

Meggie placed two fingers into her mouth and uttered a shrill whistle. John came running.

"We need to take this along." Isla pointed with a finger at the body.

"Yes, my lady," John said, without even blinking.

"Is my brother at home?" Isla asked Falks, the butler.

"Yes, my lady. His lordship is in his study."

Algie was in his study indeed, sitting behind his desk, engrossed in the business of peeling an orange with his pocketknife.

Her beloved big brother was growing old; it shot through Isla's mind. He was nearly twenty years older than her, so maybe that was the natural course of things. His thick, brown hair was receding and turning grey at the temples, and he'd developed a distinctive paunch. He looked staid, proper, and respectably middle-aged, with a golden monocle over one of his eyes. Algie was not her brother in blood, but in mind and spirit. He played the role of father, friend, and brother rolled into one. She'd loved him to bits from the moment he pulled her in his lap in London, after he and Mother had picked her up from the orphanage, sobbing, shivering, utterly terrified, and he'd said: "Do you know what pixies look like?" And that had been such an unexpectedly ridiculous thing to say in the situation that her tears had dried and she'd looked up at his face, astonished, to see whether he was serious. He was utterly serious.

"They look exactly like you." He'd tugged at her little red braid that looked more like a rat's tail. "Little and tiny as a bug. A pixiekins." The name stuck, and that's what he'd called her ever since, and she'd adored the ground he walked on.

Isla now stood in front of Algie, twisting the ribbon fastening of her overdress between her fingers. She cleared her throat, once. Twice. "Algie."

He looked up. His watery eyes brightened when he saw her. "Pixiekins." Then his face fell. "Oh no. Whenever you look like that, it's clear you've been engaged in mischief. What did you do now? Break a window? Insult a suitor? Laugh at the King in public? Out with it." He offered her a slice of orange.

Isla took a slice and bit into it, a burst of sour and sweet flavour filling her mouth, to delay her answer.

She chewed, swallowed, then said, "I think I may have killed a man." She paused to let the words sink in.

His hand paused in the act of peeling the orange only for an infinitesimal fraction of a second, before he resumed. "Have you now?"

"I'm afraid so." Now that she'd confessed, she felt light-hearted with relief.

"That's not the thing to do at all." He adopted the same avuncular tone that he used whenever he lectured her after she'd done something bad, like steal the footman's wig or eat all the sugar plums in the pantry when she was younger.

"I'm afraid not," Isla said with true remorse in her voice.

He set down the pocketknife and folded his hands on the desk. "And how exactly did that come about?" He looked at her searchingly. Sometimes he'd look at petitioners like that when they presented their cases to him. It was a sudden, razor-sharp look that cut through all one's defences.

"With my umbrella." She looked at him anxiously.

He merely blinked once. "With your umbrella."

"Well, yes. I pierced his stomach," she made a movement to show him how she did it, "and there was an alarming quantity of blood." She had to make sure he understood the gravity of the situation, for it irked her that he remained so calm. "He is quite dead."

"Where?"

"In St Giles. I went there to visit the poor." That was only half the truth, but it would have to do for now.

"Ah." Algie weighed his head back and forth. "St Giles. Then of course it is perfectly understandable why you had to kill a man." He continued to peel his orange and ate another slice, utterly composed.

Isla stared at her brother. "Algie."

"Yes, my dear?"

"Is this all you have to say?"

He looked at her with tired eyes. "What else would you have me say?"

Isla fell into the chair across from him. "What else do I want you to sa—Algie! Don't you want to know why I was in St Giles rookery in the first place?"

"It's not that big of a mystery, my dear. Another fruitless search for your Jem, I suppose?" He looked at her with weary affection. "It's quite a futile endeavour, I am compelled to note, this entire search of yours. It has always been. So I have said for years, but you must do what you need to do." He sighed.

She snapped her mouth shut.

"An endeavour that was unsuccessful, judging from the depressed expression on your face," he continued. "An endeavour that merely ended in you killing a man." He did not reprimand her, chide her, or rant that she now had lost her reputation forever. He did not threaten to lock her into her room or forbid her to ever visit St Giles again. He didn't even reprimand her for going there in the first place. Instead, he kept feeding her orange slices.

Isla took the offered slice, chewed and swallowed. Then she said, "Sometimes you just leave me speechless, brother." She regarded him thoughtfully. "Especially given the fact that you are actually a rather important person in this country."

He looked up, mildly interested. "Am I, indeed?"

Isla shook her copper-red locks, exasperated by her brother's indifference. "You are one of the most powerful, if not *the* most powerful man in this town, this country, this entire British empire!" She took a big breath. "You are not just anyone. You are this country's Home Secretary."

He meditated on her words as if that piece of information was news to him. "I am, am I not? Dash it if I hadn't forgotten for one moment."

"Algie!" Isla looked at him in exasperation. In moments like these, she doubted that her brother, Algernon Clyde, Lord Wynthorpe, was the brilliant, powerful, ruthless politician everyone thought he was. He'd single-handedly reformed the Home Office and whipped legislation after legislation through Parliament with a speed and tenacity that no predecessor had ever accomplished. The prime minister bowed to him, the Prince Regent feared him, and the ministers' knees knocked together when they had an appointment in his office in Whitehall. Behind his back, they'd given him the nickname of 'Deathmark', for his deadly aim whenever he shot a pistol. They also called him 'The Bloodhound of Whitehall' for his fearsome reputation in tracking down criminals. But Isla knew better.

Algie was no bloodhound. He was a lonely puppy seeking love and attention. He loved pruning roses in the garden, eating oranges, and was forever on a quest to grow his special orange tree. He loved going to the opera to see the Magic Flute, only to see a single aria, sung by the glorious Angelica Catalani, to which he wept, and then left. He was a terrible coward when it came to love, and because of that, an eternal bachelor who was doomed to be hopelessly in love with Lady Catherine Redgrave, a beautiful widow and Isla's best friend. Rather than confess his love to her friend, he preferred to adore her from afar.

This sweet, helpless, kind, lovable person, in short, was her brother, Algie.

"It is your duty to keep the citizens in this country safe," Isla lectured him. "Your sister confesses she killed a man in St Giles and all you do is keep eating oranges?"

He set down his pocketknife with a sigh. "What do you want me to say? If you killed him, I daresay he must have deserved to be killed."

Isla kept staring at him with an open mouth.

Algie finally took pity on her. "You say he is dead?" His chair scraped on the floor as he pushed it backwards.

"Well, let's have a look at the fellow. Let's go to St Giles. I'll tell Falks to get the carriage ready."

"That's unnecessary." Isla cleared her throat. "Because he's upstairs." In an afterthought she added, "On my bed."

He looked at her blankly. "Repeat that?"

"I had him brought home to have him cleaned up and to give him a decent burial. I thought it was the least I could do, having basically murdered him in cold blood." Isla smoothed the folds of her dress. "I thought it unclean to have him laid out on the table in the servant's hall, because, you know, people eat there. Since the guest room is currently occupied by Aunt Agatha, I gave orders for him to be brought to my room."

Finally, she had his undivided attention. "He is in your *bedroom*? You brought a *man* to your bedroom, and he is lying on your *bed*? Heavens, Isla. Have you no sense of decorum at all?" Finally, he exploded.

Isla was almost relieved but then thought with some indignation that her brother was somehow missing the point.

"He's dead," she clarified. "Perished. Extinct. A cold corpse. He's been bleeding a bit over the Aubusson carpet, and I daresay the silken bedsheets are now ruined. The maids will have substantial work washing out the blood from the sheets, but I think that sheets are replaceable. Lives aren't, even if they are those of criminals. Even though he may have been a criminal from the rookery, a sad sort of character, he deserves a proper burial. That's why I brought him here."

11

Algie's eyes nearly bulged out of his head. "Show me."

Isla threw the bedroom door open, and Algie pushed into the room behind her. Both stared on the bed, which, save for some rumpled sheets, was empty. In the open window, the curtains fluttered lightly in the evening breeze.

Chapter Two

"MY DEAR," Algie said heavily. "Your cold and dead corpse seems to have taken flight. I may be mistaken, but to my knowledge, men don't commonly walk after they're dead. I must say, I am not pleased."

Isla's scanned the room hectically. "It is rather puzzling. He definitely was dead, you know." Isla interrupted herself with a frown as the impact of his words sank in. "Algie. Don't tell me you'd have preferred there was a dead man on my bed than a live one?"

Algie polished his monocle and set it on his nose again with a frown and surveyed the scene with narrowed eyes. "Given the circumstances, yes. If, that is, you ever happened to find yourself in such a situation. Knowing you, if you had killed a man, it would more than likely be inadvertent." He began pacing the room, gesturing with one hand, as if holding a speech to a room full of MPs. "Let me guess. In the search for Jem Fawe, you entered the rookery with your maid. You attracted all manner of unsavoury attention, a cad singles you out to be fleeced, because, why not? When there is such a delicious lamb presenting herself for the offering. He probably wanted to steal a kiss, too. Because believe it or not, you are rather pretty. You pull out your umbrella which you always carry with you, jam it into his stomach, he stumbles backwards and hits his head on the stair or wall. There is blood. You think he's dead. Maybe he passed out for a while. You bring him home. You come to inform me. In the meantime, he gets up, cheerfully loots the room and jumps out of the window. He led you on. Inspect the room for any missing articles. This is a very typical sort of thing for you to do, Isla, for murder in cold blood isn't something my sister is capable of, as much as she likes to think she is. And even if you had killed him, it would have been a case of a man killed in self-defence.

Even if it had not been self-defence, if you ever happened to commit a cold-blooded crime for whatever addle-brained reason, I would of course help untangle you from that situation, because I'm always on your side. But that point is moot since that scenario will never happen. But a live, breathing man in your bed? One you put there willingly?" He pursed his lips and shook his head with disapproval. "My hands would be tied. There is nothing whatsoever I could do about that. Not to mention that it is not something I could ever countenance. Think of the scandal," he huffed. He considered the matter settled.

Isla stared at him. Her brother had told her in so many words that even if she were a criminal, he would help her. Because he was always on her side. She felt tears well up.

"Algie." She sniffed, swallowed, and dabbed at the corner of her eye. "Have I told you lately that you're the absolutely best brother in the entire world?"

"Not nearly often enough, Pixiekins. Not nearly often enough." He grunted. "Now where was I? I was doing something important. Ah yes. I must return to my oranges." He stopped at the door. "Why not let the maids clean up the mess while you continue reading to me from that new novel? What was it called again?" He snapped his fingers. "*Persuasion.* I have had a terrible day at work and must find out whether the heroine finally works up her courage to confess her feelings to the hero. There is something about the story I seem to identify with."

"Gladly," Isla said as she wiped her nose with her handkerchief.

ISLA HAD READ ALOUD for an hour from *Persuasion* until Algie started to nod off in his armchair. She looked at the sleeping figure fondly, got up and picked up the plaid that had covered his knees but had fallen to the floor. She shook it out and out fluttered a piece of paper—a despatch that Algie had been studying and that must have been entangled within the folds of the plaid. She picked it up. Just as she was about to place it on his desk, she paused. It was a letter written in cramped handwriting, interrupted by a fleeting sketch.

Isla couldn't resist. Her gaze swept over the lines.

MY LORD,

The wolf insignia has been appearing with increasing frequency throughout town, marked upon windowsills and doors of private residences, business establishments, and public houses alike. There can be no doubt: it is the emblem of Lucian Night, the notorious head of the largest criminal enterprise this country has ever known.

I await Your Lordship's instructions as to what is to be done next.

Your Lordship's most obedient servant,

Etc etc

THE SIGNATURE WAS a scrawl she couldn't identify.

Isla brought the paper close to her eyes and squinted at it.

There was no doubt, the sketch was that of a wolf; a shaggy one with his teeth bared in a snarl. Ferocious and terrifying.

She studied the drawing uneasily. It wasn't the ferociousness which bothered her, but the familiarity of it.

Where had she seen it before?

Twice, to be exact.

Once...in that narrow alley in St Giles. Didn't the man she'd stabbed collapse against a door that bore such an emblem? It'd been painted on the wood with stark red paint. Except given the situation—Isla had been convinced she'd just killed a man—she hadn't paid too much attention to it.

And then, she'd seen it again. More recently, afterwards.

Isla dropped the paper with a gasp as she remembered.

That man! The dead one. He'd been unshaven, his cheeks smeared with soot, hair escaping the kerchief tied around his head, with greasy strands falling into his face and over his eyes. He'd worn a loose, patched-up coat and threadbare trousers.

Isla shuddered at the memory.

The sleeve of his linen shirt had been pushed up to his elbows, and he'd had that emblem engraved on his forearm. Isla had stared at it, curious, as the man lay on her bed, before it occurred to her that she ought to speak to Algie, and she'd left the room.

So that Wolf tattoo was an emblem of the largest criminal enterprise in England.

Led by none other than Lucian Night.

Isla swallowed. Even she, Lady Isla Rothvale, who moved in a world of glittering ballrooms, charitable visits, and refined society, so far removed from the criminal underworld that she ought never to brush against it, even in conversation, had heard of this infamous figure.

He had many nicknames: The Undead, because he'd been hanged, but miraculously survived the incident. The King of the Devil's Drawing Room, because he controlled the most notorious gaming hells in London. The Widowmaker—that was self-explanatory. They said the number of corpses he left in his wake, even in passing, could stack as high as St. James's itself. And lastly, The Lord of Rogues, because, simply, there wasn't a bigger rogue in all of England than Lucian Night.

The man she'd stabbed with her umbrella must have

been in league with this villain. Maybe he was his understrapper or minion. Maybe he even knew him personally.

A soft shiver ran down Isla's spine.

Not that it mattered, because the man was gone, and now she would never know whether he was, indeed, in league with the Lord of Rogues.

She placed the paper on the desk and finished covering Algie's knees with the blanket.

He shifted and muttered in his sleep.

Isla smiled involuntarily and gently tucked a stray lock of grey hair out of his face.

Then she returned to her own room to turn in for the night.

To HER GREAT SURPRISE, the maids reported that nothing was missing. "All the jewellery and the coins are still here," Meggie claimed. They had scrubbed away all bloodstains, changed the sheets and aired the room. Isla had had a handful of coins lying on her dressing table. They were untouched. Her pearls were there, her diamond rings, and brooches. Everything was meticulously counted and accounted for.

The only mystery was why Lady Isla's hairpiece was so dishevelled. Crafted from her own hair, it had been carefully arranged into an elegant chignon she wore to balls. It had been placed on her dressing table. "Well now, looks like someone's gone and pulled out a few strands." Meggie scratched the back of her neck. "How odd." Then she shrugged and put the piece, or whatever remained thereof, away.

"Thank you, Meggie," Isla said, now more thoughtful than ever.

Algie had ordered additional security guards stationed around the house and in the garden, and all the locks would be exchanged the following day.

Only after she'd gone to bed, struggling to fall asleep, did it occur to Isla that Algie must have been briefed on the entire incident: her expedition to St Giles and her subsequent return with a corpse—either by the coachman or the footman, or possibly even Meggie, for she knew that Algie had informers everywhere. She wouldn't be surprised if even her abigail had joined their ranks. So, by the time she'd sought him out in his study, he must have already been aware of what had happened. Hence his lack of surprise. She was annoyed that it hadn't occurred to her earlier.

Algie had never asked outright what she'd wanted in St Giles to begin with.

But he'd been right. She'd wanted to find Jem Fawe.

They'd gone to the Angel Inn to ask whether they'd ever heard of a Jem Fawe.

"Aye," the innkeeper had said. "I knows of at least a dozen of 'em Jems." He'd winked at her salaciously. "Who's 'e to you?"

"A good friend," Isla had replied, truthfully. A childhood friend, in fact; a boy who had once been her entire world. She wouldn't be alive today if it hadn't been for him.

When she'd enquired further, the innkeeper had revealed that there was indeed a Jem Fawe working in a gin shop in Gin Lane.

"'E's lying," Meggie had warned her after they'd stepped out of the inn. "It's a trap."

But Isla had wanted to make sure. They'd ventured deeply into the heart of the rookery, and truth be told, it was amazing that they'd gone as far as they had, alive, without having been accosted by anyone, until, of course, that cad had jumped out at them.

Isla sighed.

So much had happened that day, and all in vain.

"Where, oh where are you, Jem?" she murmured as she tossed and turned, and then finally fell into a fitful sleep.

"You have to go with them, lelori," Jem had told her, but she'd clung to him, sobbing. Lelori was Jem's endearment for her. It meant little sparrow in the Anglo-Romani language.

"I don't want to," she replied in his language. "Let's go away together and find Lazlo's kumpania. He'll take us in."

Jem looked over the heather field, his eyes troubled. Then he shook his head. "He won't. He doesn't want us. You need to go with them, the gadje. They want you. They've come specifically for you. This is your chance to leave this horrible place. They will give you a home and a new name."

"But I don't want them! I don't want to live with the gadje."

"They are your people," Jem said kindly but firmly. "It is time for you to return to your own way of life."

"I don't want to leave you," she cried. "I belong with the Romani as much as you."

"I will find you," Jem had whispered. "I swear on my life. Meet me by the sundial. In Kensington Gardens."

She had waited and waited...

He never came.

ISLA WEPT IN HER DREAM. When she woke, in the middle of the night, she was disoriented. Her bed was too big, too soft, too suffocating. After all this time, she still preferred to sleep on the hard ground, for it was safe, and she missed the smell of the moist earth and dewy grass in the morning. Sighing, she threw her pillow and blanket to the ground. She climbed from her bed and lay down on the blanket. There, she fell into a fitful sleep.

The next morning, Isla awoke late, nearly at noon-time, to the sound of Meggie's scolding.

"She's doing it again! Her ladyship is sleeping on the ground again," she heard her say to Annie, the abigail.

She rose with dark rings under her eyes and with dampened spirits. Algie would return home for his nuncheon, and she usually joined him in the dining room then.

Whitehall, where the Home Office was based, lay only a short distance from their residence in St. James's Square, and on some days, when he felt especially weighed down by his duties, he insisted on walking to and from his office, to clear his mind. He particularly enjoyed his morning stroll through a small stretch of St. James's Park, savouring the quiet before stepping into the demands of Whitehall. Isla liked to join him for a light midday meal, since it was the first meal of the day for her, whereas Algie partook of something more substantial, usually mutton, beef, or pigeon pie.

Algie sawed at his beefsteak with concentration while Isla sipped her tea.

"That's right," he suddenly remarked. "Meant to give you this." He reached into his breast pocket to retrieve several sheets of paper, folded together, and handed them to her.

"What's this?" Isla took them and unfolded them.

"Since you go out of your way to scour the rookery to find your man." Algie sighed. "This is to prove it's all futile, Pixiekins."

Lists and lists...of Jem Fawes. Next to each name was an occupation and a neat mark made in ink.

Jem Fawe—butcher; Whitehall. (Marked)

Jem Faa—peddler; Southwark. (Marked)

"Goodness! How many of them are there?" Isla exclaimed.

"Hundreds." Algie set down his cutlery. "In London alone, hundreds. These are all the Jem Fawes we could find. I have hired a man solely for this task." He spread his hands. "It is worse than trying to find a needle in a haystack. As you can see, none of them is our man."

"And the check means that...?"

"...That it's not him," Algie explained patiently. "We even investigated different spellings of the name. As you know, there are variants—Fawe or Faa. It is a common name among the Gypsies. One of the oldest names there is."

"He's Rom. Romani," Isla murmured absent-mindedly. Jem had been fiercely proud of his heritage.

"Yes. But, Isla. How long has it been? Nigh twenty years?" Algie shook his head. "It's admirable, really, the tenacity with which you refused to forget the fellow."

It was true. She never forgot him. Not for a minute. Not for a second.

"Mind you," Algie continued with a dry chuckle. "When I think back to all the troubles we had to go through, Mama and I. You were so little, and we couldn't let you out of our sights. You sought every opportunity to run away to be with your Jem again. When the front door was open, you'd flit through. You nearly ran into a mail coach once."

Isla barely remembered that. Her memories from her earlier time with Algie, right after she'd left the orphanage, were blurred and she could no longer distinguish whether it had really happened, or whether she'd dreamed it all.

"The first time you ran away was when we made a stop at the inn. The footman opened the carriage door and off you went like a shot, running like lightning up the road that we'd come down, crying, 'Jem! Jem!' Had a devil of a time running after you. Caught you eventually at the next intersection. You were sobbing wildly." He shook his head. "And Mama was so upset to see you so sad; she was sobbing right along with you. That was a ride to London, I tell you, I shall never forget it."

"I made life quite difficult for you at first, didn't I?"

"Not only at first." Algie chuckled. "You sought every opportunity to look for Jem. You asked every Rom we passed whether they knew Jem. Then, after you finally grew up into a lovely lady, you stopped talking about him, and Mama and I hoped that maybe finally you'd forgotten that poor devil." He heaved a deep sigh. "Only to find that you'd developed a soft spot for charity cases and seeking every excuse to venture to Seven Dials to find Jem. It was worse than finding a needle in a haystack, but you wouldn't give up."

Isla chewed on her lower lip as her eyes dropped to the list in front of her. "Are you certain that none of them is Jem?"

"I am certain. If you ask me, three things could have happened to the fellow." He lifted a finger. "One, he rejoined his people and is travelling freely again—who knows where. He might even be on the Continent, impossible to track."

It was a possibility. There was nothing Jem had wanted more than to return to his people. He could have left the orphanage at any time, but he had stayed only to keep her company. He hadn't wanted to leave his *lelori* alone in that terrible place. He had stayed only to protect her.

She felt a lump in her throat.

"Secondly," Algie lifted a second finger. "He got transported. I'm sorry, but you know that's a common fate for the Romani, especially if they fall into crime. The law is singularly harsh against them. For many, it is a crime simply to be born Romani."

Isla nodded. "Yes. But never Jem," she said fiercely. "Jem would never become a criminal. And thirdly?"

"Thirdly," he said heavily, "he has already paid for whatever crime they accused him of."

Isla stared at him for a moment, before the meaning sunk in. "You mean he might have been executed."

"It is possible. More than possible. How else do you explain his complete absence from these lists? I've employed the best runners to help." He shrugged. "Nothing. Look, Isla. If I cannot find him, then no one can."

Isla's shoulders slumped. He was right. Her brother was the Home Secretary, after all. They called him ' 'Bloodhound'. There was no other person in all of England who was better qualified to find him. And if Algie couldn't...then who could?

She'd gone to the sundial in Kensington Gardens day after day, year after year. In vain. He'd either forgotten about her entirely, or more likely, something had happened to him that had prevented him from meeting her at the promised spot.

Maybe he really got transported.

Maybe he really was dead.

Isla stared into her tea, feeling utterly depressed.

The door opened, and Falks entered, bearing a missive on a salver. "The mail has arrived, Your Lordship."

Algie took the letter, opened it, and cursed under his breath as he read.

"You must excuse me, Isla. I have much work to do. This Lucian Night is proving to be immense trouble. He's ubiquitous, yet elusive. His network is massive. Everyone claims to know him, yet no one has truly seen him. It is as if he were a phantom. Confound it, it is most vexing." He threw down his serviette on the table.

Isla's head snapped up. "Lucian Night? His name is spoken in every drawing room. I daresay...oh, I daresay that man would know vastly more people in the underworld than you do, would he not?"

"It is possible. Now, if you will excuse me." He got up and strode to the door. "Oh, by the by. There is this fellow waiting for you again in the foyer. I passed him earlier. The one who is so smitten with you. What was his name again? Lindsay. Linfield. Lin-something."

"Lord Thaddaeus Linwood," Isla replied absent-mindedly.

"Linwood. That's the man. His tenacity in courting you is admirable. Be nice to your suitors, Isla, I beg of you." There was a mild expression of exasperation in his pale blue eyes.

"I'm always nice to them."

Algie snorted. "Rumour reached me you sent one poor fellow on a fool's quest for some impossible-to-get flower that doesn't even grow in England. Fellow was said to have nearly drowned in a lake to find it. That wasn't Linwood, was it?"

"Hm."

"Isla?"

Her head snapped up. "Oh. It might have been Linwood, indeed. It was meant to be a joke. Only he was foolish enough to take it up as a real quest. No idea how he came to fall into a lake, however. How witless of him if he did. I believe that part to be an exaggerated rumour. You know what the *ton* is like."

Algie shook his head with an exasperated sigh. "Be nice to him, Isla. He is a good man."

"Hm."

"I would like to see you married, one day. It would be nice if at least one of us wed." With those words, he finally left.

Isla remained sitting alone in the dining room, a steep furrow appearing on her forehead. "Lucian Night," she repeated thoughtfully. He certainly sounded dangerous. "Lucian Night." She tapped a pale finger on the tabletop. "Lucian Night..."

The man who was omnipresent. The man who was known by everyone, and who, likely, knew everyone, too.

Maybe he was the one who could help her find Jem— if Algie could not?

"I must find Lucian Night," Isla said under her breath.

Chapter Three

How DID one find the Lord of the Underworld when one was a respectable spinster, on top of being the sister of a prominent politician in England? It was a tricky combination, Isla concluded, as she stepped out of the dining room into the corridor.

The eyes of society were perpetually upon her, and what was worse, there was her brother. Algie must never uncover her true plans, nor could she afford to be caught —ever!—for that would land him in the gravest of difficulties. She could cause him serious trouble, the kind that might endanger his political career, and Isla would never allow that to happen.

Whatever she did next, she would have to tread with extreme caution.

The real problem, Isla mused as she stepped down the stairs, was being a lady. It came with so many restrictions. One perpetually had to keep up appearances, plus, being unmarried, she had to take along chaperones wherever she went. It was most inconvenient. Isla, however, believed that at her advanced age of twenty-six she ought to finally be well beyond that requirement. How very vexing it all was! It certainly wasn't easy being a spinster.

"Lady Isla!" A cheerful voice hailed her from below. "I have been waiting for you these past few hours."

Thaddaeus Doxford, Lord Linwood, stood at the bottom stairs, a bouquet in his hand, beaming up at her as if she were the Goddess Aphrodite personified.

"Lord Linwood. How do you do? I receive callers at three o'clock in the afternoon, as you well know by now," she reprimanded him gently, for it seemed as though his morning calls came earlier every day. Indeed, one day he might turn up before noon, when all and sundry knew that morning calls were supposed to be held in the afternoon.

She led him to the drawing room, leaving the door open, and gave instructions to the butler to fetch her Aunt Agatha as a chaperone.

Linwood followed her eagerly. "I do know, Lady Isla, and I beg your pardon for appearing at this untimely hour, but I had a most urgent reason for this visit."

Linwood wasn't particularly tall; he had a well-proportioned figure with an athletic frame and was a full head smaller than Algie, but she was of such petite stature that she still had to tilt her head up to look into his face.

Like always, he was dressed immaculately in a plain brown suit. His dark hair was slicked back to reveal a well-formed forehead, and he pushed his horn-rimmed spectacles up his nose with his finger. It was a mannerism that was peculiar to him, a tick that Isla observed with amusement. Sometimes she counted the number of times he did so during a conversation. And it was particularly amusing when he did so in the ballroom, while dancing a lively reel.

"What was so urgent?" she enquired, indicating with one hand for him to sit at the sofa near the window.

"This." He held the flowers beneath her nose. "The rare blue orchid. I have found it, Lady Isla. I have completed the quest. I have discovered the rarest and most beautiful flower in existence, for the rarest and most beautiful lady in existence." With a flourish, he presented it to her with a bow.

"Goodness! So you did." Isla blinked at the flower, utterly baffled that Algie had been right. It had been a fib. She had invented the name of the flower in a moment of caprice, merely to rid herself of his excessive attention at an Almack's ball. She had never expected him to take her jest in earnest, let alone succeed.

Accepting the pot from his hands, she examined the delicate blue blossom. It was beautiful, indeed, its petals a deep, rich indigo, so vibrant it seemed almost unnatural.

"How extraordinary!"

"Yes. It was brought back by Dr Griffith from Hindustan. It is said to grow in the deepest reaches of the jungle, and he brought back a specimen and continued to grow it in his glasshouse in Wiltshire. I ventured to his estate to acquire one. I overcame several obstacles in order to do so." He adjusted his spectacles.

"Like falling into a lake?" Lady Isla enquired cautiously. "Never tell me those rumours are true?"

The colour in his cheeks heightened. "Err. I might

have made acquaintance with Dr Griffith's lake in the erroneous assumption that the flower was found on the island within it. The little rowing boat had a leak and then I lost my balance...Dr Griffith corrected my false assumption, of course, after he fished me out of the lake and lent me a change of clothes. Imagine that, Lady Isla! It turned out his glasshouse wasn't located on that island after all, but behind his mansion."

"Indeed." Isla set down the flower and crossed her arms over her chest. "You seem to have had quite an adventure." She briefly wondered where Aunt Agatha was and why she wasn't here yet. If she was napping, Falks would have a devil of a time waking her.

"Yes. It was my pleasure. I would do anything for you, you know." He looked at her with a soft expression on his face.

Isla repressed a sigh. She had many suitors, and it normally wasn't difficult for her to turn them down. But this one, this Lord Linwood, for some reason was. Not only was he the most persistent, but he was also so—what was the word? Naïve? Innocent? There was something childlike about his manner, something refreshing about the honesty of his emotions, that made it difficult for her to reject him. His eyes were huge behind his glasses, a melting, trusting, chocolate brown.

Like that of a puppy.

And Isla had a weakness for little children and puppies. The trouble was that Linwood reminded her of both.

"I am most grateful," Isla said gently. "It is one of the most beautiful flowers I have ever seen and knowing of its origin and how difficult it was for you to acquire it, I shall tend to it most carefully. Thank you."

He beamed at her happily. "I can get more for you, if you want."

"It is quite unnecessary," Isla said hastily. "One is quite enough, thank you." She glanced at the clock on the mantelpiece. "But goodness, time flies. I have some appointments..." She hoped he would take the hint and leave.

Linwood followed her gaze and frowned. "It isn't correct."

Isla blinked. "I beg your pardon?"

"The time. It isn't correct. It is now," he pulled out his pocket watch. "Twelve fifty-eight, to be precise. The clock there is two minutes behind." He stepped up to it. "May I?"

"By all means," Isla said after she found her voice.

He set the clock to rights, turning the key in the back. "There. It is now correct. I have also noticed the Horse Guards Clock in Whitehall is running a minute behind. I dared not mention it to your brother when I met him earlier, but it has been bothering me. What if he runs late because of it? It is important for clocks to be accurate. Clocks are my passion, you see. Do you think you could mention that to your brother? That the Horse Guards Clock isn't accurate, and he should not trust it, I mean."

"By all means." Isla lifted a hand. "Thank you for caring about my brother's punctuality."

Linwood flashed his white teeth at her. "He is a very busy man, after all."

"Certainly." She nodded at him and turned to the door.

"Lady Isla."

What now? She paused and turned.

"Will you marry me?"

He stood at the other end of the room, by the fireplace, his face as anxious as ever, as if he hadn't asked that question—Isla made a quick mental calculation—thirty-five times already.

The first time had been not an hour after they'd first been introduced to each other at Almack's. He'd asked her for a dance; it had been a Cotillon, and immediately after, on the dance floor, he'd asked her to marry him. She'd brushed him off with a laugh.

She hadn't known then that he'd been sincere.

The very next day, he'd called upon her with a bouquet of roses, and repeated his proposal, right in the presence of Aunt Agatha, too, who had been snoring in the armchair by the window.

She'd brushed him off once more, and sent him to Algie, reminding him that he had to first acquire her brother's permission to court her. She'd hoped that having to do so would have deterred him, for it had deterred many suitors in the past. It was surprising how many men had slunk away and were never seen again as soon as she'd uttered those words. Not that she'd minded; but it had always irked her somewhat.

To her surprise, Algie had told her the next day, at breakfast, that Linwood had called on him, requesting his permission to court her. Algie had sent him right back to his sister, saying that it all depended on her, and that she did not need his permission.

"I've never seen a man so terrified," Algie had grumbled. "And I've seen my share of terrified men. Do him a favour and accept his suit before he dies of terror."

Isla had dropped her spoon. "Never say you look favourably on his suit."

"Of course I do. One of us must marry, and it had better be you. Linwood's a ninny, but he's of good stock. He'll suit you well," Algie had said before he'd buried himself in his newspaper.

Since then, Linwood had shown up with a persistence that had been nothing short of remarkable. He'd ended each visit with a proposal, which she'd turned down firmly, but politely, and always with a twinge of conscience upon seeing his downcast face.

Thirty-five proposals.

This was the thirty-sixth.

Isla furrowed her brow. Her hand froze on the door. Her thoughts raced. Then, before she could change her mind, the words were out: "Very well, then. Yes."

"Because you would make me the happiest of—" He interrupted himself. "What did you say?"

An involuntary smile crossed her face at the utterly flabbergasted expression on his. "I said yes. I will marry you, Lord Linwood."

His jaw dropped. "T-truly?"

She lifted an eyebrow. "You did mean it, did you not? Your proposal. Was it sincere?"

"I am—Of course—Yes! But—You said yes? You will

truly marry me?" He stepped forward, stumbled over a low stool that was in his path, and gripped the back of the armchair to steady himself.

"That is what I said." Isla nodded. "As of now, we are betrothed."

Then she saw something rather astonishing.

Lord Linwood smiled.

It was an authentic smile that lit up his eyes deeply from within, as though the sun of Spain was rising over a barren field. His dark eyes lit up and glowed. And two delicious little dents formed on his cheeks, one to either side of his mouth.

Isla stared at him, speechless.

The man, truly, had dimples! It was almost outrageous how adorable he suddenly looked.

"I am—" He was visibly searching for words. "Happy." He finally settled on one. "I am so happy. Truly happy," he stammered, entirely incapable of finding a different kind of word that expressed the same sentiment.

That drew an authentic smile from Isla. "I am, too," she said softly.

Oddly enough, it wasn't even a lie.

He raised his hands to his head, as if he still could not believe his luck, took a few steps forward, then back again, took off his spectacles and then put them back on again with a flurried movement. "What happens now? What to do? The banns. The trousseau. The church. A wedding date. The settlement. So many things." He looked at her with round eyes. "Your brother!"

Isla nodded. "I daresay the next step is to inform my

brother. And then to settle on a date. Shall we agree, uh, half a year hence?" That was long enough for either of them to change their minds, Isla reasoned.

"Half a year? But that is far too long." Linwood shook his head. "Must we wait that long?"

"Oh, very well. Five months?"

"Two months?"

Isla shook her head. "Three."

Linwood's countenance fell.

"And you need not worry about the trousseau. Usually, the bride takes care of that," she added quickly. "But for now, you must talk to my brother."

He nodded. "Your brother, then. Must talk to your brother. At once." He jammed his hat on his head and rushed to the door. He stopped, returned, bowed. "I shall return," he promised, bowed again, then left for good.

Isla shook her head as she watched him rush out of the house.

"Isla." A thin voice sounded behind her. Isla turned. Aunt Agatha had finally come down the stairs, leaning on a footman's arm, a tad too late. "I was told my presence as a chaperone was needed."

"It is kind of you, Aunt, but that is no longer necessary."

Her aunt nodded. "In that case, I shall return to my nap."

"Aunt, I am to marry Lord Thaddaeus Linwood," Isla said. "You are the first to know."

Her aunt nodded, entirely unsurprised. "That is excellent, child. Do you love him?"

That took the wind out of Isla's sails. "Love?"

"Well, yes." Aunt Agatha looked at her with unaccustomed sharpness in her eyes. "You wouldn't want to marry a man you don't love."

Isla spluttered. "I—er—I believe it shall not be difficult." She cleared her throat. "He has a very lovable character." That, at least, was true.

Her aunt nodded again. "Love is all that matters. Regardless of what they say. Do not settle for anything less than that."

Isla watched silently as her aunt, with the help of the footman, resumed her slow climb up the stairs back to her room.

Maybe Isla had committed a folly, accepting Linwood's proposal like that.

But, oddly enough, she didn't regret her impulsive decision one bit.

It would be exceedingly advantageous to have a man to whom one was engaged, Isla mused. Particularly Linwood, who would attend to her every whim. He would be entirely at her bidding, which would be most convenient.

She could always break it off later. And even if she did not, it might not be so dreadful to be married to Linwood. He would be ever at her beck and call, and there was something to be said for being wed to a man who all but carried one on his hands. By consenting to this engagement, she had bargained herself a measure of freedom, however modest it might be.

Algie would be lulled into believing she was well taken care of, while Linwood, blissfully unaware, would become her unwitting ally, protecting her, accompanying her in public, in the search for the Lord of the Underworld. And no one would bat an eyelid.

Isla rubbed her hands.

It was an excellent plan, indeed.

Chapter Four

"You did what?"

Lady Catherine Redgrave, widow of the late Marquess of Redgrave, set aside the silver pincers she had been using to shape her brows into a fine, elegant arch and turned to stare at Isla. Draped in a pale pink satin negligee, Catherine had been in the midst of her morning toilette when Isla had announced herself. But as bosom friends, they had long dispensed with formality, and Isla knew Catherine was best approached at this hour before she began her visiting rounds about town.

Isla tugged at the lace fichu at her throat, as if to compose herself, succeeding only in making it more askew.

"I said," she repeated, "I have at last accepted Lord Thaddaeus Linwood's proposal."

Catherine's brows, one perfectly shaped and the other yet unfinished, drew together. "But my friend. My dear, dear friend." She let out a slow breath. "Why?"

Isla crossed the room and sank onto the settee by the

window. "Three reasons. No—four." She lifted a hand, fingers poised to count them off.

"Firstly, because it will be convenient to have a gentleman at my side during my inquiries." Catherine, of course, knew of her efforts to locate Jem. "He lends me a measure of propriety. A lady alone in the less reputable quarters of London invites speculation, perhaps even censure. But a lady accompanied by the man she is to marry? That raises fewer brows. People may still take note, but it places a veil of respectability over the matter, enough to divert attention from Lady Isla and her so-called eccentricities."

Catherine studied her with a critical eye. "And the second reason?"

"Safety. On my last visit to the rookery, Meggie and I were attacked." Isla folded her hands primly in her lap, as if that might somehow diminish the gravity of the admission. It did not.

"I have thought more than once that it would be wise to have a male accomplice, so to speak, someone whose mere presence might deter petty pickpockets and, more importantly, assaults. I am a wretched shot." She made a mental note to inquire whether Linwood had any proficiency with a pistol.

"Linwood, while not precisely a Corinthian, knows a thing or two about boxing. He mentioned training with Jackson. I do not think he is a heavyweight, but," she lifted one shoulder in a half-shrug, "it may prove useful one day."

Catherine eyed her shrewdly. "And why not take a footman along? Or two, for that matter?"

"For a very simple reason," Isla explained patiently. "Every last one of my brother's servants, save for Meggie, reports anything I do or say directly to Algie. That simply will not do."

She hesitated just a moment before pressing on. "Which brings me to my third reason: Algie himself. Thus far, he has been remarkably patient and even, dare I say it, supportive of my efforts."

Catherine nodded. "He truly is a saint of a brother. I cannot think of another man who would turn a blind eye to his sister's highly eccentric, if not outright reckless, escapades." Her gaze sharpened. "You do realise, do you not, that you are not only endangering yourself but also him? With every one of your excursions, you risk his reputation."

"I know." Isla bit her lip.

Catherine leaned back, her expression turning contemplative. "You really do have a wonderful brother."

"I do." Isla seized the opportunity to heap further praise. "He is wonderful, understanding, and caring. The best brother a person could wish for."

Catherine's only response was a knowing glance.

Undeterred, Isla pressed on. "But that, you see, is precisely the issue. After what happened the other day, Algie's patience has reached its limit. He will never say as much, but I can tell. And now, he has begun to speak of marriage."

Her friend's head snapped up.

"He very much wishes to see me married," Isla clari-fied. "By getting engaged to Linwood, I relieve him of that particular concern. It will allow him to believe that Linwood shall take charge of me now."

"So you may carry on with your mad schemes undisturbed."

"Precisely." Isla smiled.

"And the fourth reason?"

"If I must become engaged," she said with a careless wave of her hand, "it may as well be Linwood. He is neither the brightest candle nor the quickest wit."

"Ah. I see. And this, too, is an advantage?" She lifted a fine eyebrow.

"Absolutely." Isla's eyes glinted. "A man who does not dazzle with his intellect is unlikely to prove difficult. He will do as I say, and I shall hold the reins in that particular arrangement."

Catherine's lips twitched. "How very clever of you."

"What is more," Isla continued, warming to the subject, "he is one of those rare men who do not seem to mind when women flout society's expectations. Not because he is radical or liberal, but simply because he does not care. He is far too absorbed in his own world— books and some peculiar interests that no one else follows —to trouble himself over such matters."

"That does seem accurate," Catherine said with a nod. "He is from an excellent family, very respectable, yet he is not much concerned with what others think or do. He is quite singular in his ways."

"More than that," Isla mused, "he is entirely indifferent to society's rigid rules. And do you know why?" She leaned forward slightly. "Because he himself is so different, so removed from the rest. He will never seek to control me." Her voice softened. "Just as Algie never has."

Catherine tilted her head. "You almost sound as though you like him."

"Like?" Isla's brow furrowed. "Do I like him?" She considered the question with genuine curiosity. "I certainly do not dislike him. We get along well enough. He is not the most accomplished dancer, but then, neither are many men. He is a bit of a bore and has a tendency to expound at length about his interests,"—she waved a dismissive hand—"which range from geology, clocks and even lepidoptery. But it is not altogether unpleasant to listen to, because some of it *is* interesting. He is so passionate about his odd little fascinations, it is almost..." She paused, searching for the right word. "Endearing?"

"You do like him." Catherine's lips curled into a triumphant smile.

Isla waved a hand dismissively. "I rather think it is the other way around. He has proposed thirty-five times. Or was it thirty-six?"

Catherine's eyes met Isla's in a frank gaze. "Never say he is in love with you?"

A faint pink hue crept across Isla's cheeks. "Nonsense. I simply happen to suit him."

Catherine let out a "hm," her expression unreadable. "You have almost convinced me. But tell me, are you truly sincere about this union? Or do you intend to cry off?"

Isla grimaced. "At first, I thought I could always withdraw if it became too tiresome, but I am beginning to suspect it may not be quite so simple." She gave a small shrug. "If he proves to be a useful companion, then there is no reason not to proceed. A husband who does not seek to control me might be rather convenient, after all."

Catherine nearly dropped the hare's foot she'd picked up earlier. "Your cold-blooded pragmatism almost shocks me." Then, under her breath, she muttered, "Poor Linwood."

Things developed quickly from then on.

The next day, Algie informed Isla that Linwood had, in a most unorthodox move, appeared in his office at Whitehall, to formally ask for her hand.

He'd specifically made an appointment with his secretary for that purpose.

The wedding was to take place two months hence.

"In two months! Already!" burst from Isla. "Hadn't we agreed on three?"

"Linwood is quite impatient," Algie replied with a frown. "He would have preferred it to take place within a fortnight but accedes to your wishes of waiting longer. Two months was my suggestion. While I am glad that you finally accepted his suit, I hope you did not feel pressured into it based on our conversation the previous day. Why do I have the feeling you accepted his suit so readily simply because I suggested it?"

"Certainly not, brother. I merely thought about it and decided that you were right. One of us ought to marry. Since it's not you, then it had better be me." She buttered her roll and bit into it with gusto.

He grunted, and there was a slightly dissatisfied expression on his face.

"And since I am bravely setting an example, it only seems right that you follow suit. I think you should finally talk to Catherine."

"I did talk to her," he said, in between two bites of mutton pie. "I met her in the park yesterday. I said, 'How do you do, Lady Redgrave?' and she replied, 'Very well, thank you, my lord.' And then I said, 'Fine weather today, is it not?' and she said, 'Truly my lord, it is. Though it looks like it might rain soon. It is a shame I forgot to bring my umbrella.' Which is a most puzzling utterance if you consider that there was not a cloud in the sky. And she kept her eyes fixed on my umbrella the entire time." A look of anxiety flitted through his eyes. "What do you think she might have meant with that? Do you think it might have a hidden message? That possibly she wasn't so pleased to see me, after all?"

"Oh, Algie," Isla groaned, resisting the urge to bang her head against the dining table. "Didn't you say you brought your umbrella?"

"Of course I did. Just like you, I never leave the house without one, regardless of the weather. But I do not see what that has to do with what Lady Redgrave said."

Isla sighed. "It was an invitation for you to walk with her in the park."

His watery blue eyes looked at her helplessly. "This does not make any sense whatsoever."

"Must I explain it plainly? She said she was concerned about the rain. Never mind whether it was a reasonable concern and whether it really would have rained or not. That is not the issue. But, as a gentleman, you should have offered to walk with her, since you have an umbrella."

He shook his head. "I still do not follow."

"So you can share the umbrella with her in the eventuality that it does rain!"

"But the sun was shining brightly and there was not a speck of a cloud in the sky! Why the deuce would she need an umbrella?"

Isla threw up her hands. "Forget the umbrella! Of course it was not about the rain at all."

"You are just like the MPs I have to argue with daily. You're making less and less sense, saying one thing, meaning another, and contradicting yourself in a single sentence. Just like Lady Redgrave." He huffed.

"Algie." Isla schooled herself to be patient. "A lady like Catherine can hardly say to a man like you, 'My lord, will you spend some of your precious time with me and take a walk with me through the park? I would dearly love to take a walk with you.' This, Algie, is what she really meant to say."

Algie blinked. "Then why didn't she just say so to begin with?"

"Because she can't!"

"Why ever not, by Jove's beard?"

"Because she is a lady! We ladies can't possibly take the initiative and issue invitations to gentlemen. It is most excessively improper, irksome as it is! We must always wait for the gentleman to take the initiative. I can't tell you how exasperating that is. I shall enjoy very much not having to do so anymore, now that I am engaged to

Linwood. But that is neither here nor there. And secondly, it is because you are you, because of your person! You are far too important. You can't just ask the Home Secretary to take a stroll with you through St James' Park. It just isn't done."

He scratched the back of his neck. "So, you are saying it was not about the rain at all, but merely an excuse. And that she wanted us to take a walk together. How excessively...confusing. How is one ever to understand the double meaning of things?"

"Practice, dear Algie, practice. If you would but speak more often to the opposite sex, you would learn that things, in fact, aren't all that complicated at all. But it is something which you obstinately refuse to do."

"I do not like small talk. Particularly with the opposite sex," Algie mumbled. "I simply do not know how to do it."

"True. Though I must say," Isla said more generously, "if one considers that fact, you did very well, to be sure. You uttered two grammatically correct sentences to Catherine. That is so much better than the animalistic grunt you uttered last week, at the charity ball that she organised, when she asked you whether you enjoyed yourself and liked the ball. Truly, you hurt her feelings. Today, you actually spoke like a civilised human being. So very well done, Algie. Remarkably so." She clapped.

Algie gave her an exasperated look. "I'd better stick to my work. That at least is something I understand."

"Yes." Isla chewed thoughtfully and swallowed. "Say, Algie. About that man, Lucian Night. Why don't you simply have him arrested? Wouldn't that solve all the criminal problems we have and clear the city of crime?"

He folded his hands on his stomach in front of him. "If only it were that easy. Night is as elusive as a shadow, one moment here, the other gone. He was caught once. Do you know the story? You may have been too young to remember."

Isla leaned forward. "The one where they hanged him, but he somehow escaped? I thought that was merely a legend."

"It was true. Ten or so years ago, he was caught, put on trial, sentenced to be executed to be hanged until dead. On the day of his execution, all of London came to watch the event. The executioner did his job, and the man swung from the gallows. It was a short drop."

Isla pushed the plate away, suddenly having lost her appetite. "And?"

He shrugged. "When they cut him down, they discovered he was still alive."

"Good heavens."

"Precisely. You wouldn't believe the uproar it created. The crowd clamoured for him to be pardoned. Which the Home Office eventually agreed to. Fearing the crowd's anger, and with all the political upheaval going on in the country, riots and what not, it was what they decided to do. I would never have done it, of course, if they had asked me." Algie shrugged. "But I was not Home Secretary back then."

"And what happened afterwards?" Isla asked, breathless.

"He turned into a legend overnight. Disappeared,

and when he reappeared, he was even more powerful than before. Brought the entire underworld under his command, of which he is now the self-appointed overlord."

"Until you catch him." Isla propped both elbows on the table thoughtfully. "Which you undoubtedly will, sooner or later."

"That much is certain. But it isn't so easy. The world of crime isn't as organised as one would believe it is. There are hundreds of gangs, not all of them allied, many fighting each other, with new ones being created daily. They have one thing in common: they all swear allegiance to Lucian Night. With the exception of one, and one only: the Mudlark Skulls."

"The Mudlark Skulls! Who are they?"

"Pirates and smugglers who are involved with a pernicious human trafficking ring who appeared suddenly on the Thames. They steal people from the streets and sell them as slaves in the new world. They are the only ones who are currently challenging Lucian Night's authority. Aren't you reading the papers? They're full of this."

"Why read the papers when I can get everything directly from the source?" Isla retorted sensibly.

Algie got up. "This is, at any rate, what occupies me the most these days. While Night is kept busy with the pirates, his attention is elsewhere. This is a good time for us to strike."

"And then he will be hanged. Again." Isla tilted her head. "I wonder whether he will stay dead this time."

"That, my dear Pixiekins, is a given." And with a nod, Algie left the room.

Lord Thaddaeus Linwood was waiting for her in the hallway—again.

Again, he held flowers in his hand.

This time, they were pink carnations. "They stand for affection and deep admiration," Linwood told her as he handed her the bouquet with a flourishing bow. "Says the flower vendor."

"Thank you, my lord." She smelled the bouquet before handing them to the footman to put into a vase. "You have appeared in the timeliest manner, today," she told him as she put on her bonnet. "Let us go on a ride together?"

"Gladly." He beamed at her.

Isla gave instructions to the coachman, then Linwood helped her into the carriage. "Thank you, my lord."

Linwood looked at her shyly. "Don't you think, now that we are to marry, that you could call me something else, maybe? Please call me Thaddaeus."

"Thaddaeus." She tried the name on her lips. Then she shook her head. "No. It is far too serious a name for you. I'd call my grandfather Thaddaeus, but not my betrothed. Don't you have anything less formal? Any nicknames?"

He pushed up the spectacles on his nose. "Nicknames?"

"Yes, you know—my brother has several nicknames,

even. Other than 'Bloodhound of Whitehall' and 'Death-mark'. 'Windy'—short form for Wynthorpe. I call him Algie, even though his name is Algernon. But it's too much of a mouthful, so nicknames are perfect for names like these."

"My classmates at Eton used to call me Woody," he said with some hesitation. "But I don't like it at all. It was always followed by the sensation of having my head dunked into a chamber pot. 'Woody look!' and then—" He made the motion of having his face pushed into a chamber pot.

"They did not!" Isla exclaimed. "How horrid of them! Is this the life you had at Eton?"

He shrugged. "I survived it."

Isla gave him a pitying look. "Did you never defend yourself?"

"I did," he nodded. "I became good at running away. I became so good at it, I was the fastest runner in the entire school."

Isla could imagine it. A little, younger version of Linwood, scrawnier, being chased around the courtyard by a group of bullies...

She shook her head. "But we were discussing nick-names. You are right, I can hardly call you Woody, or Linnie." She pulled a face. "Don't you have other kinds of nicknames? Affectionate ones."

He shook his head.

"I see I shall have to invent one, then." She thought for one moment. "Thaddaeus. Thad. Tad. Ted." She pursed her lips. "None of that fits. Ted, maybe. Ah! I have it! Teddy."

"Teddy?" His face was so comical, she burst into laughter.

"Yes, Teddy is perfect. It suits you perfectly. I shall call you Teddy. In private only, of course. In public you shall be Linwood, prim and proper as always. And you may come up with a nickname for me as well."

He stared at her. "Isla. It is a beautiful name. I couldn't possibly call you anything else. It is sacrilege."

"Pooh. How unimaginative you are. Algie calls me Pixiekins."

"Pixiekins," he exclaimed. "Truly? A mythological being?"

Isla burst into laughter. "Not exactly, but an invented one. He meant to suggest something small, quick, maybe mischievous."

"Hm. Like an insect." He made a thoughtful face. "I shall have to come up with something similar, then."

He pondered on the matter during the entire carriage ride.

"I have it! How about book louse? The plural being book lice, but since there is only one of you..." His voice petered off.

"Book louse? As a nickname? It is hardly affectionate, don't you think?"

"I suppose not. I was thinking because you like books..."

Isla pulled a face.

"What about earwig? Or mantis. There are also chequered beetles—" he said eagerly.

"No insects," Isla interrupted hastily. "Please."

"I shall have to think about it and come up with

something affectionately appropriate that you, too, will like," he said as the carriage came to a halt.

"Do so, Teddy," Isla said. "Though it is quite acceptable if you just keep on calling me Isla. Shall we, then?" The footman opened the door, and she descended from the carriage.

"Lovely weather today," Teddy said, cheerfully offering Isla his arm. "Perfect for a stroll."

"Quite so," Isla retorted, taking his arm with one hand and gripping her umbrella tightly in the other. "Let us take a stroll, then. There is an incredibly rare clock in this neighbourhood that I'd like to show you. I think you'll find it quite fascinating," she said as she directed him into the heart of the rookery that was St Giles.

Chapter Five

IT HAD BEEN an excellent idea to bring Teddy along to St Giles, Isla decided. The man was, on one hand, hopelessly enamoured with her, and on the other, so utterly engrossed in explaining the intricate workings of clocks that he was blissfully unaware of their surroundings. He saw nothing at all peculiar about strolling through the most disreputable alleys in London; not as long as he had Isla by his side and an attentive audience for his lecture on horology.

Teddy chattered away, absently twirling his walking stick, as he launched into a detailed discourse on the clock of St Paul's; why it was considered one of the finest public clocks of its time, and precisely how its weights and gears functioned.

"The clock is driven by weights, created by the clockmaker Langley Bradley in 1708, who was an absolute genius, if you ask me. There is possibly only one other clockmaker who might be an even greater genius, and that is Thomas Tompion. His timepieces set the standard for precision, and while the clock of St Paul's is accurate, we all know the clocks at the Royal Observatory in Greenwich by Arnold and Harrison are even more precise. But as for sheer elegance and innovation in clock-making, no one surpassed Tompion. But then, one wouldn't expect anything less from the finest clockmaker England has ever known."

He paused mid-step, as if struck by inspiration, and glanced down at her with sudden enthusiasm. "I would love to show you a Tompion clock one day!"

"You know an awful lot about clocks," Isla mentioned absent-mindedly as she studied the doors of the crooked little houses in the alley. Now, where was that door with the wolf emblem?

"Yes, I do," Teddy replied. "For the greatest part of my life, I would have loved to become a clockmaker myself. I even studied with John Roger Arnold for a while, the finest chronometer maker of our time, although some may argue that that may have been his father."

Isla lifted her head. "You wanted to become a clock-maker? In truth?"

He nodded. "Yes. But you know how it is." He shrugged. "Duty of our class and whatnot. My father wouldn't have it, so it had to remain a mere passion. These days, I like to tinker around with clocks whenever I can find the time, which is precious little. I have even transformed an entire room to a worksho—ooff."

A scruffy boy shot out of a side alley and barrelled straight into him, taking the wind out of his sails. Teddy staggered back from the impact. His walking stick flew out of his hand and clattered on the ground, and his other arm shot up in a swift, protective motion, half-sheltering her as he turned to face the boy.

The boy scrambled to retrieve the stick on the ground, and would have, no doubt, run off with his prize, when he froze, dropped it as if it were a piece of hot coal, and scrambled backwards on the ground, on all fours, away from them, until he hit the wall of the house.

"I am so sorry," he babbled. "I didn't mean it." He kept repeating those two phrases, except the language he spoke was not English. "I didn't know. I am sorry."

"Eh?" Teddy picked up his stick and brushed it off. "What are you saying, boy?"

Isla recognised the language. "What didn't you know?" She crouched down by the boy, answering in his language. "Tell me."

But the boy kept shaking his head, trembling. "I am so, so sorry," he repeated. Then he scrambled up and, before he ran off, threw some items at Teddy's feet.

"Eh," Teddy repeated as picked up his silken hand-kerchief and his purse. "That little wretch stole my hand-kerchief, my purse and my stick. Except he seems to have thought better of it. Very honourable of him." He searched his pockets to check whether there were more items missing. "He didn't filch my fob and pocket watch. Maybe because both are attached to my waistcoat." He patted his pocket watch in relief. "Otherwise, I tend to lose them or place them somewhere, you know."

"That was...most peculiar," Isla observed quietly. She

turned around, but behind them was merely a stone house. The shutters were closed. She scanned the building with a frown. "Excessively odd behaviour. What was it that the boy saw that frightened him so?"

"The hangman's noose, most likely," Teddy replied as he cleaned his spectacles with his handkerchief and pushed it up his nose. "Are you well, Isla? You're not hurt? He did not steal anything from you?"

Isla shook her head. "I am fine, and I still have all my belongings." Her fingers gripped her umbrella as she cast a nervous look down the dark little street.

"Say, it has occurred to me for quite some time already that this appears to be a rather peculiar place for a walk. The people here do not appear to be too friendly," he commented, as if only now becoming aware of their surroundings. A window shutter slammed shut above them as they looked up, which caused Isla to flinch.

What Isla found even stranger was that, save for the encounter with the boy, they didn't actually meet anyone. The shady figures that she thought she saw in the corners and doorways melted away as they approached, so that, blinking, she decided she must have imagined them. There were no beggars on the ground, no drunkards skulking along the walls, no ruffians threatening to relieve them of their valuables.

They were in the middle of Gin Lane, one of the most crowded, filthy, dangerous alleys in all of London, a street where they said that once you entered it, you were unlikely to leave alive, and no soul was to be seen. As soon as people saw them approach, they disappeared in the doorways, houses, and shadows, as if the very air had swallowed them whole. Only the wind blew several lonely stray leaves along the ground, and a cat hissed and spat at them as they passed by.

There was something wrong.

Growing increasingly nervous, Isla pulled her shawl tighter around her shoulders. Gripping Teddy's arm, she dragged him along the alley, trying to remember where the place had been where she'd stabbed the man. The narrow streets looked so similar, and it was difficult to remember where exactly it had been.

"Where is that clock that you wanted to show me?" He paused, looking around.

"We're close. Was it here?" she said to herself, as she pulled Teddy into a narrow side street. It did look vaguely familiar.

"Clocks aside, I find this a rather curious place to find oneself," Teddy commented. "Lots of gin sold here." His face brightened. "Here they are, the clocks." He pointed with his stick at a dilapidated pawn shop. Through the dirty shop window, one could see an assortment of pocket watches. "Is this what you wanted to show me?" He studied the items displayed in the window with great interest. "Some of these are interesting specimens."

Isla smiled brightly. "Indeed." It was a lie, naturally, for dragging him to St Giles to show him a clock had been merely an excuse; but the pawn shop appeared at a convenient time.

Teddy pulled out his own watch. "Most of them are punctual, too," he praised.

Isla was about to answer that these watches were,

likely, stolen goods, when her eyes fell on the door next to the pawnshop.

There it was.

The red wolf.

She gasped.

This was the place. There were the stairs where she'd stabbed the man. He'd staggered backwards and crashed against this very door.

After a moment's hesitation, she lifted her gloved hand and knocked against the door.

No one opened.

"Did you want to visit the pawnshop? The door is over here," Teddy said, pointing at the door on the other side. But the moment he'd uttered that, a sign in the window appeared, saying it was closed. "But it is closed," he added, frowning.

"What do you make of this?" Isla pointed at the emblem of the door.

"It's not a friendly image, is it?" Teddy tilted his head to one side, then to the other. "Is that blood dripping from its fangs? A vampyre, mayhap?"

"Not quite. It is a wolf. Though now that you mention it, one can't help but wonder whether that association was intentional. Haven't you seen this emblem before?"

He bent down to squint at it, then shook his head. "Can't say that I have."

Isla tapped a finger against her cheek. "It's the third time I've seen this image within two days. I must say, I'm curious. I'm very, very curious. And, as you should know about me, if I'm curious about something, I don't give up until that curiosity is satisfied. I can be more stubborn than a bulldog locking its jaw around a piece of meaty bone."

Teddy looked at her, awe-struck. "Truly? How very useful to know—I mean, since we're to marry, and all, it is useful that we know of each other's traits. I tend to be similar. If something arouses my curiosity, I spend hours in the library until I find the answer." He regarded the wolf again and scratched the back of his neck. "It does look rather fearsome."

"Yes." She narrowed her eyes as she studied the wolf. "That must have been intentional. What do you think? Could it be the emblems of smugglers? To brand their contraband with? Or a secret code used by criminals? Should we find out?" She knocked again, but once more, no one answered. "Could you bang against the door with the handle of your walking stick, with all your might? It would be louder than my knuckles."

Teddy did as she requested, and it worked: after three thumps against the door, it finally opened with a creak.

A greasy-looking, half-bald man with a dirty apron tied about his waist stood in the doorway. Isla recoiled, thinking the stains on the apron were bloodstains.

The man looked at them suspiciously through narrowed eyes. "Yes? What d'ye want?"

Teddy, who had his hand lifted in the process of knocking a fourth time, lowered his cane, and took an involuntary step back.

The man stared, and his face transformed. He backed away and attempted to slam the door shut again, but Isla had the presence of mind and placed her foot into the threshold.

"What d'ye want?" he repeated, his eyes flitting from her to Teddy and back again.

"Just one question," she said hastily.

He backed off into the shadows of the house, so that she could no longer see his face.

"The sign on your door. The wolf. What does it mean?"

The man did not reply.

"What does it represent?" she insisted.

The man's eyes shifted to Teddy. He hesitated, then mumbled something.

Isla shook her head. "I don't understand a word."

"I said, it's the sign of our leader."

Isla's pulse started to increase. "Leader? Who?"

The man mumbled something she couldn't grasp.

"Answer," Teddy said quietly.

The man cast him a fearful look. "Lucian Night."

Isla exhaled slowly. She'd known, of course. This was a confirmation that she was on the right track. But she needed to go one step further. "Is this where he can be found?" she pressed. "Does he live here?"

But the man slammed the door right into their faces.

Isla made an annoyed exclamation.

"Strange man," Teddy commented, taking her arm to lead her back to the carriage. "Not exactly of the communicative sort. That's as far as your curiosity will be satisfied."

Isla frowned. She hadn't really learned anything that she hadn't known before. And she hadn't come a step closer to Lucian Night. "How vexatious," she mumbled.

Teddy cast her a sideways look. "He wasn't a very savoury character at all. And if he is in league with Lucian Night, then it is best we leave these premises as fast as possible before he sends some thugs after us." He cast a nervous look over his shoulder.

Isla sighed. "Yes. I suppose you are right."

"I learned quite a bit about my bride to be this afternoon," he conversed cheerfully. "I daresay, some of it is most surprising."

Isla repressed a sigh. "Is it?"

"Yes. You have the most peculiar interests, I must say. Taking walks in the most disreputable areas of London, for one. Is it a habit? It is rather uncommon, wouldn't you say? Unless there is a reason, of course." He stopped as if an idea had occurred to him. "Pray, are you on a quest of some sort?"

Isla stumbled over her boots. "Err. No. Why would you think that?"

He shrugged. "It just occurred to me, that is all."

"It is merely curiosity, like I said." She chewed on her lower lip before continuing. "I enjoy exploring the less fashionable parts of London, you know. What else is it that you discovered about me?" she asked, to detract his attention from the subject they were discussing.

"You speak the language of the Rom." He gave her an appraising look. "How extraordinary."

Isla's knuckles tightened over the handle of her umbrella. "Yes. Well." She thought hard before she managed to come up with an answer. It couldn't be helped. She had to tell him the truth. "I suppose you ought to know. As a young child, I lived with the Rom for about two years."

Teddy stopped in his tracks. "Did you, now? You mean, you lived with the Gypsies and travelled with them all over the country?"

"Yes." She frowned. "I owe them my life. They found me amongst the wrecks of a carriage accident. My nurse was dead, and I was barely alive. I was five years old. If they hadn't found me and nursed me back to health when they did, I would have died as well. They were my family. I stayed with them until Algie and my mother found me at the orphanage." She'd left out many details, but Isla thought that that was as much as Teddy needed to know for now.

Teddy's eyes were warm and sympathetic. "As I said, how extraordinary."

"I thought Algie might have told you."

"He did not."

"Well, now you know. Also, that Algie and I are not related by blood. My mother took me in because she wanted to have another child. But she was not my biological mother. My true father was the former Marquess of Ellhall. He died in the Flanders campaign."

"And your mother? Lady Ellhall, I mean."

Isla's eyes drifted into the distance. "She died at my birth. The current marquess who inherited not only the title but the land and the house where I was born does not acknowledge my existence." She shrugged. "It honestly doesn't matter to me, as I don't consider him to be my family. The woman I consider to be my true mother is Lady Wynthorpe. I loved her dearly until she passed away three years ago." A look of sadness flickered over her face. Then she cast him a self-conscious look. "Will you...that is, knowing all this now, do you still want to marry me? My background is rather dubious."

He blinked. "Naturally. I don't see what one thing has to do with the other. I don't care a fig's worth for what society thinks and whether you and Wynthorpe really share the same blood, or not. It is immaterial."

A feeling of warmth flooded through her.

"He is my family. The only one I have," Isla said simply.

Teddy nodded. "And I am your future family."

Again, that feeling, this time more sizzling. What on earth was that?

"Thank you for sharing your story with me, Isla."

They reached the carriage, and he helped her inside. "It has been a most interesting afternoon," Teddy said conversationally. "I must return to buy some of those pocket watches. Some seemed to be very rare. I wonder whether that pawn shop is owned by that man as well. Lucian Night." He grimaced. "Wouldn't want to cross his path. Though I wouldn't be worried about crossing his path there," he added as if an afterthought.

Isla's attention perked up. "What do you mean?"

"All and sundry know Night owns a disreputable gaming hell in Covent Garden." Teddy shrugged.

Isla shot up in her seat. "Do you know the name of the gaming hell?"

"The Club of the 101, most likely," Teddy said easily, pushing his spectacles up his nose. "It goes by another name, too: The Scarlet Wolf. It's not a secret at all that the owner of that club is Lucian Night. After they get tired of White's, the men usually flock to the Wolf, where the real stakes are wagered."

Isla gaped at him. "Truly?"

He squinted at her through his spectacles, but because the sun reflected in his glasses, she couldn't make out the expression in his eyes. "Is this why we came here? To find Lucian Night? I could've told you if you'd asked me."

Her eyes shot up to meet his. She had to be careful. Teddy wasn't at all the empty-headed nitwit he gave the impression of being. He would need some explanation as to why she brought him here. She decided on a half-truth. "I saw the sign on one of Algie's documents. Then, again, elsewhere." She could hardly tell him it had been tattooed on a man's arm, a man she'd stabbed, and who'd been lying on her bed, to boot, could she? "When I saw the emblem on the door, I felt the urge to investigate." She gave him a mischievous look. "I am my brother's sister, after all. Call it a family trait."

Teddy nodded, as if it was a perfectly valid explanation, and Isla heaved a sigh of relief.

"Though I find it quite perplexing if Night is known to be in Covent Garden, why Algie is having such trouble arresting him." That did truly puzzle her.

"I don't suppose men like Night are as easily found as that. He probably has a hundred disguises."

Isla looked at him with large eyes. "Does he?"

"But enough about that unsavoury character. You spare no effort in your endeavours, do you?"

She gave a small shrug. "When I commit myself to a cause, I do so with great zeal."

"It is one thing I admire so much about you, Isla." His smile was warm. "And now I know your nickname, too. You said nicknames were supposed to be affectionate but a little silly. Therefore, I shall call you Lala." He looked very pleased with himself.

Isla burst into laughter. "Lala. Very well. Teddy and Lala. What a curious couple we shall make."

He grinned. Then he sobered.

"What?"

"I was just thinking...since we are engaged now..." He looked at her bashfully.

She returned his regard with amusement. "Yes?"

"Whether it might be all right for me to hold your hand." There was a blush creeping up his cheeks. "Only if you want."

Isla suppressed a smile and gave him her hand.

He took it reverently.

Then, ever so slowly, he began to ease the glove from her hand, tugging gently at each finger in turn. By the time he finally slipped it free, warmth had unfurled through her, her breath had quickened, and her pulse had begun a most unsteady rhythm.

It was really quite vexatious.

His warm hand closed over hers, and for one breathless moment, she could think of nothing at all—nothing but the way his skin felt, soft and warm and impossibly smooth, as he gripped her hand.

"Do tell me, Lala, what shall we do next?"

She cleared her throat, still vexed with herself.

"Let us go to Gunter's for ices," she eventually said. It would be good to get something cool in her body, she decided.

And then, in the middle of spooning the most delicious orgeat and Parmesan ices, Isla asked, as it suddenly occurred to her, "Do you enjoy gambling?"

He shrugged. "Not particularly."

"Why?"

"Because I always win."

Her spoon paused half-way to her mouth before she lowered it again. "You always win?" she echoed.

"Certainly." He arranged his spectacles on his nose. "I was thrown out of a club once because of that."

"No. Tell me more."

He wrinkled his forehead. "It was a ridiculous situation. I kept winning, which they didn't like. They don't know it's quite easy to win. They assumed I was cheating, but it's just mathematics. If one counts the cards and calculates probabilities, it's quite simple to determine when to place a wager and when to hold back."

"Oh. They can't have been too pleased about that, I suppose."

He grinned at her. "I happen to be good at numbers."

Isla played with her spoon. "I've never been to a real gaming hell, you know. Wouldn't be the thing for the sister of Lord Wynthorpe."

He nodded sympathetically. "It's a shame, really, for gaming hells can be quite amusing, though they are not at all the thing for ladies."

She leaned forward, a gleam in her eyes. "Take me to one?"

Teddy's jaw dropped. "To a gaming hell?"

"Yes. To the Club of the 101."

Teddy's spectacles slid off his nose as he forgot to push them back up. "Certainly not. It is only for gentlemen."

She tilted her head aside with an impish grin spread over her face. "Then I shall have to dress up as one, shall I not?"

Chapter Six

It took Isla nearly an entire week to convince Teddy of her plan. She badgered, wheedled, and nudged, but he remained resolute. Only when she threatened to go with Catherine instead, both of them dressed as men and accompanied by a single footman for protection, did he finally relent. By appealing to his protective instincts, she managed to get exactly what she wanted.

Isla squealed with delight.

"I shall regret this," he grumbled. "Of that, I am certain. But what am I to do when I have not yet learned how to say no to your harebrained adventures?"

"It is splendid of you to indulge in my whims. Truly." She grabbed his arm and shook it enthusiastically.

He went pink but made no movement to pull away. He said gruffly, as if to play over his embarrassment, "We'll stay for half an hour and not a moment longer. Just so we are clear, if anyone so much as looks at you in the wrong way, I shall challenge them to a duel."

"Fear not." Isla dropped his arm. "I shall make myself

as inconspicuous as possible and tread only in your shadow. I only want a brief glimpse of that world, and then we can go."

Lucian Night's infamous gaming hell in Covent Garden masqueraded as a respectable establishment near Drury Lane. However, it attracted all manner of people, catering to both gentlemen and scoundrels alike. Actors, officers, noblemen, and wealthy tradesmen mingled freely with a more dubious clientele, whose backgrounds were unmistakably disreputable.

To Isla's great surprise, there were also women present. Many were clearly companions to the gentlemen, either wives or mistresses; however, the demi-mondaines were present as well: actresses, courtesans, and widows willing to risk their reputations. They clung to the arms of their men, watching them play, or they themselves threw the dice at the hazard table.

"If I had known that women are admitted here, I'd have foregone this disguise," she said more to herself than to her companion, who appeared clearly agitated. Yet the disguise was necessary, for it would not do to be recognised as Lord Wynthorpe's sister. The excitement of being there prickled under her skin, and she surveyed the room eagerly.

"Are you certain you want to step into this den of iniquity?" Teddy's gaze flickered anxiously around the room, sweeping over the tightly packed bodies crowding about the hazard table in the middle of the room, and the thick haze of smoke, perfume, and sweat that clung to the air. He seemed more concerned about her safety than her being dressed up as a man.

Earlier, when she'd emerged smartly dressed in breeches and an evening coat, which gave her the appearance of a young, slender man, he'd blinked at her bemusedly.

"Permit me to present myself: your nephew, Ian Roth." She made a crooked half-bow.

Teddy shook his head. "I don't know what is more scandalous: that you're dressed up as a man, or that you look more dashing in that evening suit than I do. Your cravat is crooked." He reached out to tug at it. "Remind me again why we're doing this?"

"To satisfy my curiosity." She gave him an impish smile. "I've always wanted to know what it's like, to visit a real gaming hell." Isla peeked down to watch his hands deftly retie her neck cloth. "Remember, I'm your nephew whom you've decided to introduce to the world of gambling. And it is true, it is an entirely new world to me, one which I take great delight in exploring." She wanted to leave Teddy in the belief that she was merely adventurous, wanting to learn more about the life of gambling, and that she had no other ulterior motive for being there. So far, it appeared to be working.

As they surveyed the room from the entrance, where they stood, a thrill coursed through her body. She felt with every fibre of her being that tonight she would find the answer to her quest.

"Shall we, then?"

Teddy gave a curt nod. "Follow me."

When a raucous eruption of cheers and groans

exploded in the room, Teddy stepped instinctively closer to Isla, as if to protect her.

Isla concluded that when it came to her person, Teddy's sense of safety and protectiveness was stronger than that of propriety. He didn't seem to mind that she dressed up as a boy and visited disreputable places; in fact, she was surprised that so far, he'd gone along with every madcap scheme she'd come up with, and she was curious how far he'd go. There were not many men like that. The average man would have bristled with righteous indignation and rigid propriety, and would have prevented her, if not forbidden her, from going on the grounds that it was scandalous for women. Such men would not be wrong. Isla was well aware that what she was doing was folly; if she was discovered, her reputation would be in tatters, and it would tarnish her brother's as well.

Yet Teddy hadn't breathed a word about propriety and reputation.

His only concern was that of safety.

A strange, warm feeling flooded through her.

Yes, it had been the right decision to accept Teddy's suit. If he continued to be as lenient towards her in the future as well, she would be quite glad to marry him.

He stayed close to her, taking her by the elbow, as he guided her through the room, muttering, "In the centre of the room is the hazard table. It is fast-paced and high-risk, and the main attraction of this club. I don't advise to play it because it is so unpredictable." They remained by the side, watching how the dice were cast. Isla gasped at the enormous amount of money that was wagered. Fortunes were won and lost with the casting of the dice.

"The card tables are in the next room, where they play faro and basset. They are more to my taste." They moved on to the adjoining room.

As soon as they entered, Teddy was promptly hailed by a half-drunk gentleman sitting at one of the tables.

"Woody! Fancy seeing you here."

Teddy swore under his breath. "Edgefair. It has been a while." He nodded at the man, then gestured at Isla. "My nephew, Ian Roth."

Edgefair gave her a cursory glance and a nod. Then he tossed his cards on the table. "Lost this round. Come, join us for another?"

Isla nodded at Teddy, who took a seat while she remained standing behind him. "I prefer to watch," she said in a low, gruff voice.

It was instructive watching Teddy play. He played with utter concentration; his gaze never strayed from his cards. To her astonishment, she saw that he was right about never losing. He was winning every single round.

Isla watched, intrigued. Teddy's attention was taken up entirely by the game and it seemed he had entirely forgotten that she was there.

Good.

She took a step back from his chair.

Then another one. And another.

She reached the door, turned, and melted into the crowd in the main playing room.

She scanned the room. If the owner of the club was present, within these walls, it was impossible to ascertain who he was. He could be anyone, really, Isla mused. Her eyes fell on the footmen who wove themselves between the people, carrying trays. They came and went through a door in the wall that, no doubt, led to further rooms behind the main ones. Isla watched one footman open the door and disappear behind it. He'd left the door slightly ajar.

This was her chance. With a quick look over her shoulder, Isla went after the footman.

Chances were that it would lead to the servants' staircase, and she would end up in the servants' premises below stairs. Truly, that appeared to be the case. There was the kitchen, the servants' hall, and a series of rooms that were intended for the domestics. It looked entirely normal, like in every other household.

Maybe she was naïve thinking that Lucian Night would be found within these premises, Isla thought. Just because this was his club did not mean that he lived here. Who knew how many houses he owned, who knew in what other houses he spent the night?

Quite possibly, and with increasing likelihood, not here.

Isla's shoulders sagged. She had no idea why she'd thought this was going to be so much easier than it was. Why had she thought that she could accomplish something that her brother couldn't? Why had she thought she could find him by simply walking into his club and looking for him? Isla rubbed her forehead with a sigh, uncertain what to do.

A footman came towards her, bearing a tray with glasses. He looked at her sharply. "May I help you, sir?"

"I—I got lost," Isla said in her deeper, gruff voice.

"The way back to the main room is here," he indicated with his free hand to the door through which she'd just come.

"Yes." She hesitated. "But I wanted to talk to the owner of this club. Is he here?"

The footman shifted his tray from one hand to the other. "Regarding which matter, sir?"

Isla's jaw nearly dropped to the ground. He hadn't denied that Night was here. Did that mean that he was in truth? Her mind worked furiously.

"Regarding an urgent business matter that only concerns him and me. You know." She cleared her throat. "It is confidential."

The footman gave a penetrating look. "Wait here, if you please, sir."

Isla nearly collapsed against the wall when he left. Her heart was hammering, and her mouth had become dry. She should have picked up one of those champagne glasses the footman had been carrying.

After a while, a large, burly man appeared. Isla stared at him with wide eyes. Surely that couldn't be him?

"How may I help you?"

"Are you Lucian Night?" she blurted out. Maybe that had been a mistake, but the man didn't even blink when she uttered his name.

"No, sir. My name is Holborn, the manager of this place. Do you have an appointment with Night?"

One could have appointments with the Lord of the Underworld? As easily as that? Surely, matters could not be so simple.

Isla thought swiftly. "Not exactly. But I must speak with him. It is of the utmost urgency. A question of life and death. And it concerns a business affair of great interest to him as well."

Just like the footman, the man gave her a scrutinising glance. "Certainly. If you would follow me, sir."

Isla stumbled after him, scarcely believing her success.

She was being taken to a meeting with the Lord of the Underworld.

And it had been shockingly easy.

HOLBORN LED her through a series of corridors, rooms and doors. Steps up and down, then further down, then along corridors again, then further down. It was an underground maze.

Surely, they were no longer in the same building, which had been an unassuming, narrow red brick house from the outside. Judging from the distance they'd been walking, they might have gone underground, the distance of at least five, if not six houses.

The decoration changed, as well. The light became dimmer as the corridors were more sparsely lit, and it appeared unfurnished.

Just when she was about to ask him when they would finally arrive, Holborn finally stopped in front of an unas- suming wooden door.

He nodded at her.

Isla knocked on the door gingerly.

There was no reply.

She went inside.

THE ROOM WAS DARK. There was only a single candle lit, standing on a little coffee table by the door, and next to it, a chair.

"Lady Isla Rothvale," a chilling, hollow, disembodied voice said from the depths of the room, as if belonging to a spectre. "Welcome."

Isla squinted into the darkness. He had been anticipating her.

That was strange.

Her heart was hammering painfully, and she moistened her dry lips before she said, "Who are you? And more importantly, where are you?"

"Sit down," the same voice said. "If you please."

Isla dropped into the chair. "How did you know my name?"

"I know everything, Lady Isla." Isla imagined a shadow moving at the other end of the room. Was there a desk, perhaps? Another chair? He was there, that was for sure. "I know that you have been looking for me these past few days. And I am intrigued." Isla leaned forward to catch his voice better.

"The sister of the Home Secretary personally wants to have a rendezvous with me." He sounded amused. "And her brother does not know a thing. Behold me intrigued. How could I not acquiesce?"

Isla gripped her fingers tightly in her lap. "How did you know?"

"Knowing these things is part of my business."

Of course. He must have spies everywhere. Even in Algie's office? The thought was unsettling.

"Can't you light more candles? I don't particularly like talking to shadows. Besides, it's somewhat cowardly of you hiding in the darkness, so I can't see you, while you can very well see me."

He laughed quietly, a sound that sent shivers running up and down her spine. "It would be most imprudent of me to show my face to the sister of the Home Secretary. Wynthorpe is trying his best to capture me and see me swing—again—but I will not give him that satisfaction."

"How...how did you manage to survive that?" She couldn't help it. She *had* to ask.

He chuckled. "The devil's luck, no doubt. I dropped, then the entire contraption gave way. I was unconscious, and the physicians brought me back."

The hangman must have lent a helping hand, Isla supposed. She rubbed her neck.

"Charming outfit, Lady Isla, by the by."

She felt heat rising to her cheeks, which annoyed her. She raised her chin. "I have come here on business."

"I am intrigued," the voice drawled. "In what kind of business capacity may I be of assistance?"

She leaned forward, imagining that she saw a figure moving in the shadows, but she couldn't make out anything specific. "They say you know everyone and if not, that you can find anyone."

"Who are you looking for?"

"A man called Jem Fawe."

"There are hundreds of Jem Fawes in England." That's what Algie had said, too.

"He is about thirty, but that is all I know. I don't know what he looks like. I suppose he would have dark hair and eyes, since he is half Romani."

"That is not much to go by, Lady Isla."

Isla squinted at the right corner of the room, for the voice suddenly came from there. It appeared he was pacing as he talked.

"In short, you are unable to help me."

"I didn't say that." The voice came from the other corner of the room. "If I agree to help you, it is guaranteed that I will find him. It all depends on one thing, though."

"What?"

"How high you are willing to pay for my service." The voice had shifted and somehow seemed closer. The little hairs on Isla's arms stood on end.

"How—how much would it cost?" She shifted restlessly in her seat.

"I don't take money for services like this." He paused. "But I demand payment for services rendered in a different form."

"What do you mean?"

"A pact."

It sounded sinister. Isla shivered. "As in, a pact with the devil," she retorted.

He laughed softly, and the sound made her want to jump up and run out of the room, but she gripped the edge of the stool and forced herself to remain.

"I wouldn't exactly ask for your soul, tempting though it may be."

"What then?"

"I would ask for three things."

"That seems a tad unfair, considering that my request consists of only one thing."

"It is how I conduct my dealings," the voice replied lazily.

"Very well. What three things would those be?"

"Your first waltz."

Isla blinked. "I beg your pardon. Did you say you wanted my first waltz?"

"You heard correctly."

She knitted her brows together. "What do you mean, 'first waltz'? Where? When? How? I've already waltzed, so it wouldn't be my first waltz."

"It would be your first waltz at an occasion that I would determine."

"You wish to dance with me?" she asked, incredulous. "At Almack's? Or the Argyll rooms?" That Lucian Night wanted to dance a waltz with her in public, as part of the repayment for him to help her find Jem, was the most ludicrous thing she had ever heard.

"Even if it were at Almack's or the Argyll rooms, you'd be required to comply."

Her mouth dropped. He really did mean it. Well, what of it? She'd waltzed with many men. She might as well waltz with Lucian Night.

She shrugged. "Very well. What else?"

"Excellent." She could hear the smile in his voice and for a fraction of a second wondered what she'd just agreed to. "The second point in the agreement would be another 'first'."

"I am all agog as to what that could be," she muttered.

"I want your first kiss."

Isla's mouth dropped. Then she snapped it shut. "Certainly not."

"As anticipated, this is the point where the lady draws a boundary. Then our pact will come to naught, and this business discussion is superfluous. I wish you a nice evening."

Was he mad? Or thoroughly depraved? The scoundrel was clearly enjoying himself. One thing was certain: he was a rogue. Heat shot into her cheeks, and her eyes flashed angrily. "I came here, willing to negotiate and pay handsomely for hiring your services to help me find a person. I am insulted to find that you make light of the situation by trifling with my request by suggesting such an outrageous—" she drew circles in the air with her hands "—as you call it, pact. I call it an impertinence, and that is putting it mildly."

"I am not trifling, Lady Isla, and neither am I making light of the situation." His voice had turned frosty.

Isla dropped back into her chair. "You are being serious."

"I am indeed."

"But—but why?" He could have asked for all sorts of things: money, her family heirlooms, jewellery, a pardon for one of his cronies, even intelligence from Algie's office. But he wanted a waltz and a kiss? She rubbed her cheek. It would indeed be her first kiss, since she hadn't yet kissed a man, aside from pecking quick kisses on Algie's cheek—but that didn't count. She didn't much like the notion that her first kiss would go to a scoundrel and rogue.

"What is your third request?" she retorted coolly. She had a presentiment as soon as she uttered his words. If he wanted a first waltz, followed by her first kiss, which was a heightening of stakes, that logically meant that the stakes would escalate dramatically to something profoundly shocking, and all that was left was that he'd ask for—

"Your first night."

Ha. "I knew it!" It escaped her before she could help herself.

"Your wedding night, to be precise," he clarified, as if she hadn't already known.

"I believe you mistake yourself for a medieval lord enforcing *droit de seigneur*." Isla's voice came out scornfully. Really. The gall of the man! She found herself more annoyed than shocked, though she should have been terribly shocked.

"What would you have me say?" his voice was amused. "I am known for my shocking contracts. I am the Lord of the Underworld, after all."

"Lord of Rogues would be more accurate," Isla muttered.

But she had the nagging suspicion that that was the aim of the entire conversation: to shock her and frighten her thoroughly. Why? To get her to back out? Once again, why?

"It is quite futile. My husband will have something to say on the matter as well, and I daresay he won't appreciate having a stranger in our bedroom on our wedding night."

"You're to be married to that dimwit lord, aren't you?

Linwood. He is of course a nuisance, but nothing that can't be taken care of."

Isla shook her head. "He isn't that much of a dimwit. I daresay he has the intelligence of this entire establishment put together. He is fleecing you even as we speak."

"Ah yes. Word regarding his 'luck' in gaming has gone round. Yet another reason why the man is a thorn in my eye."

Isla narrowed her eyes. "If you hurt him, our entire contract is null and void."

"Do you love him?" The question was shot at her so unexpectedly that it caught Isla off guard.

She began to stutter.

"It doesn't sound like she does," the voice said pensively.

"Be quiet," she replied, crossly. "Of course I do. Otherwise, I wouldn't marry him. I could have married anyone, you know, but I didn't want to. I care very dearly for him, and if you as much as hurt a hair on his body, I shall...I shall...personally make sure you swing at Newgate, and I'll be there, watching." The moment the words were out of her mouth, she knew they were true. The thought that he could hurt Teddy filled her with an unanticipated fury.

"Ah. The lady does seem to have developed some feelings for the dimwit lord. Very well. What about the other one? Jem Fawe? Does Linwood know you're so desperately looking for him? I gather not. What would he say if he were to find out?"

Isla bit on her lip. He did not know, and she wanted to keep it that way. "Jem is a childhood friend whom I care for dearly. I am certain Linwood would understand that I would want to find him again."

"Then why not ask him to help you find him? Why the secrecy?"

Why, indeed?

Suddenly, a confusion seized her that she couldn't explain. "I simply wish it to be so," she said lamely. "I suppose I would tell Linwood. Eventually." Or not.

Why couldn't she bear to tell him about Jem?

Because she truly loved Jem?

Always had, always would...

There was a momentary silence.

"Very well, Lady Isla." His voice sounded cold and business-like. "I am fairly certain I can find this Jem for you. But my terms remained unchanged. I want my three 'firsts'."

Isla stood up, with a lifted chin. He expected her to back out of it. She knew it. He expected her to refuse his outrageous, scandalous proposal. Maybe he wanted her to get cold feet. Maybe he did not want her to find Jem.

Yet again...why?

"Very well. I agree."

"You agree to my terms?" His voice sounded surprised, which confirmed that he'd wanted to scare her away.

"I can tell you did not really expect me to acquiesce to your terms, but I will. Should we not be signing some sort of contract? After all, verbal agreements on their own are not sufficient when conducting serious business." She took a step forward into the darkness, towards what she suspected was a desk.

"Stop," the voice shot out.

Ah. He felt threatened.

"I confess I am surprised. Lady Isla doesn't shy away from the most heinous business terms if it means that she will find her childhood love. I wonder what her husband would say to this matter."

"He is never to find out," Isla responded immediately. "Include that in the contract. I insist on absolute discretion."

"That you shall have. I shall make certain that a contract will be forwarded on to you in the next few days. Make sure you sign it."

"How will you reach me?"

"I have my ways. Await my instructions. Now, Lady Isla. I suggest you make your way back to the gaming room and rejoin your bridegroom. He must have fleeced half of the gentlemen in the card room already. How does he do it? Counting cards?"

"He uses his mind and the probability of mathematics," Isla responded.

"Ah. How exceedingly clever. It goes without saying, he will never show his face in these premises again, and neither will you."

Isla nodded. She would be glad to never set foot there again.

She wanted to turn around to say a final word to Lucian Night, but the door opened, and Holborn appeared to take her back to the gaming salon.

The room was, if possible, even fuller than it was before, the air thicker, and the people more drunk.

Teddy threw down his final card when she entered

and retook her place right behind him. She was breathless and her hand shook as she stabilised herself at the back of Teddy's chair.

He turned his cards, and a collective groan filled the room. "I won again. I think, gentlemen, that was my last game." He collected his vowels, which had been thrown on the table, and turned to meet Isla's gaze.

He smiled.

"Well done." Isla's tongue ran over her lips. It appeared he had been so engrossed in his game that he hadn't noticed that she'd been absent.

Teddy promptly began discussing the game and analysing where his opponents had gone wrong, and how he had been able to hold the upper hand. Isla nodded. "Tell me all about it on the way home? I confess I have had quite enough. It is sticky and hot in here."

Teddy agreed.

She was quiet in the carriage on the way home, while Teddy talked, until he, too, fell quiet.

"You appear worried," he eventually said.

Isla looked up sharply. "Not at all. I'm merely tired. I must say, my curiosity regarding gaming hells is satisfied, and I shall be more than happy if I never set foot in one, ever again. They are horrid places, particularly this one." She repressed a shudder.

He grinned. "Excellent. I share that sentiment. Shall we attempt something entirely different in the next few days?"

The carriage came to a halt in front of the Wynthorpe town house. The lights were on. Algie was clearly in his study, working.

"Such as what?"

"Seeking a house." His smile grew as she stared at him.

"Seeking a house?"

"Why, yes? I could hardly bring my wife to live with me in the Albany. It's strictly bachelor's lodgings."

She looked at him, perplexed. "I see." The thought of going house-hunting had never crossed her mind.

"We can look at several houses and then choose which one is most to your liking. After all, it shall be your new home soon."

Isla had difficulty wrapping her head around that notion. "Home." She would have to move out of the Wynthorpe town house.

She collected herself. "You are quite right. Yes, let us do that."

Chapter Seven

THAT NIGHT, Isla fell into bed, exhausted.

Meggie had let her in through the servant's door, and she'd slipped up into her room without running into any of Algie's servants.

She'd tiptoed past the half-open door of Algie's study, where he was sitting by his desk, perusing some documents.

Running a tired hand over her forehead, Isla wondered whether tonight's escapade had truly been worth the bother.

True, she had met Lucian Night. Or at least a man who claimed to be him.

He'd made her a very scandalous proposal. But then, that had been his intention: to scandalise her to the point of crying off.

Isla furrowed her brows. *Why?*

Would he be truly able to help her?

And now that she'd agreed to his conditions, what

would happen next? He'd said that she had to wait for further instructions.

Isla was not good at waiting.

Her thoughts wandered to Teddy, and she felt a pang of guilt. She felt she was deceiving him and taking advantage of his good nature. Had she possibly endangered him? Night had sounded threatening towards him.

Isla tossed and turned as she considered telling him the truth. But no. She couldn't possibly tell him of this pact; it was simply too outrageous, too scandalous, too shocking. Teddy had been very lenient with her; but something told her that this would push it too far. If Teddy ever knew of her agreement with that man, it would jolt even him out of his complacent obliviousness and chances were good he would object most severely. As for Algie...

She sat up straight in her bed.

Algie could never find out what she was up to.

It would be a disaster if he did.

SEVERAL DAYS PASSED, and there was no sign of Lucian Night or one of his minions. Isla was secretly relieved. Maybe nothing would come of it, after all. It had been a folly to believe that it would.

She spent her days with Teddy, visiting houses in Mayfair.

He had taken the reins in his hands, often quite literally, as they took his curricle to drive about Mayfair to visit all the houses he had on his list.

To Isla's great surprise, she enjoyed herself.

And to her even greater surprise, they seemed to share a similar taste in housing.

"I don't know," Teddy said, shaking his head, as they stood in front of a tall, morose looking town house. The windows faced north, and there seemed to be precious little light reaching the rooms inside.

Isla tilted her head sideways. "It looks somewhat like..."

"A top hat," they said simultaneously. They looked at each other.

"Tall and narrow and black. It's the black brick." Teddy pursed his lips. "I don't think we need to visit the rooms inside, do we?"

Isla shook her head. "Shall we pause for some refreshment? We've visited enough houses this morning."

Teddy agreed. He took her to Gunter's.

"My life's philosophy is that there can't be enough sugar in one's sweetmeats." Isla studied the menu card and sighed. "If only I could make up my mind! How excessively difficult it is to make a decision. Should I try the Parmesan again, or Gruyère? Or opt for something fruitier, like the barberry one?"

"Maybe we don't have to make a decision," Teddy said. "We could just try them all."

To Isla's laughing protest, Teddy ordered the waiter to bring a sample of each of the flavours that were on offer. Their table was laden with small bowls filled with different flavours, including chocolate, peppermint, violet, rose, bergamot and even orgeat.

Isla was utterly transported.

They argued playfully over which was the best

flavour. Teddy tended to prefer the salty, spicier ones, and Isla the sweet, flowery ones. Both agreed that the Gruyère was too strong, however, and the rose one too sweet.

Teddy set his spoon aside, claiming he'd had enough ices to last the entire Season.

"I would like to show you my estate," Teddy said after the waiter had cleared the table. "It's in Yorkshire, by the coast. The mansion is set on top of a hill with a view over the sea. I called it Roseview Mansion. I think you'll like it."

"I can't wait to see it," Isla said softly.

Teddy pulled out a small velvet pouch and, after a moment's hesitation, pushed it across the table. "This is for you. I have been carrying it with me for quite a while already."

"What is it?" Isla took the blue velvet pouch in her hand and opened it curiously. She took out a small, round, golden pocket watch. It lay warm in her hand. The cover was engraved with a pretty paisley pattern. It was a blue enamel watch with inlaid pearls and diamonds.

It came with a beautiful golden cord.

"You can attach it to your waist, or wear it around your neck," Teddy said gruffly. "And it is the most accurate pocket watch in this entire kingdom. I personally made sure of that. I commissioned the case, but made the inner clockwork myself."

Isla gasped. "You did? How extraordinary," she said as she turned it in her palm. She flipped the lid open and marvelled at the delicate dials that indicated the hours. How on earth had he done it?

"I designed it myself. Do you like it?" He looked at her anxiously, as if her answer mattered greatly.

"It is the prettiest thing I have ever seen." She smiled. "And now I have no excuse to ever be late again."

His face broke into a relieved smile. "It is my engagement present to you." He looked at her shyly. "I know it should have been a ring. I shall buy a ring, too. But I thought a watch was more...practical."

"It definitely is," Isla said cheerfully. "And I don't need a ring. It will forever get in the way. I like to take off rings and misplace them, and then I lose them. No, I prefer this. How thoughtful of you! Thank you so much." She beamed at him. "I shall have to think of something to give to you in return."

He waved it away. "You need not give me anything except your time and presence. That gives me the ultimate happiness." His gaze was warm, and a brown lock of hair fell over his forehead, making him look boyish.

Isla blushed and searched for words. Why did she suddenly feel so tongue-tied? This was Teddy, for heaven's sake.

Teddy, who suddenly made her blush.

"We are going to the opera tonight, are we not?" To her relief, he changed the topic.

"Yes. Something by Rossini." Isla rose. "I shall wear this watch tonight and time the length of the opera."

Teddy grinned at her, and her heart skipped a beat.

Chapter Eight

It happened at the opera.

They went to the King's Theatre to listen to an Italian opera: *Rossini's Il Barbiere di Siviglia.* Algie had a box, even though he himself excused himself from the night's performance, claiming he was too busy. This was despite Isla telling him that Catherine would be there.

For one moment it looked like he wavered, but then he gave a determined shake of his head. "Not tonight. I have some urgent business to finish. Besides," he pulled a face, "Rossini is not to my taste."

"Ah yes, you only listen to a single aria by Mozart and then leave afterwards." Isla smirked.

If Catherine was disappointed because Algie didn't join them, she did not let it show. She was dressed in a beautiful night blue gown and she looked young and vivacious. Isla was pleased with her own green silk dress, her copper red hair swept upwards and fastened with an ivory comb. She sat between Catherine and Teddy, leaning eagerly over the balustrade of their box to follow the opera on stage.

Isla was entirely engrossed in the wonderful music. Once or twice, she laughed out loud, her eyes wandering to Teddy, who was watching her more than the stage. He looked splendid in his dark blue tailcoat and breeches. His hand inched towards hers, closing around it in a firm grasp. Isla froze. He held on just a moment longer, his gaze averted, yet a mischievous smile teased at the corners of his lips. An answering smile tugged at hers. She let herself relax. Though layers of fine gloves separated them, the moment felt strangely intimate, almost clandestine. Here they were, holding hands in the midst of an opera, unseen and unnoticed by anyone but themselves. It was improper, daring, and utterly thrilling.

Isla was reluctant to release him when the intermission came, and Catherine turned to them with sparkling eyes. "Wasn't that wonderful? I vow, I have never seen a better performance."

"It was splendid," Teddy said. "Particularly the stage design and the props. I liked the fact that they used real clocks. I noticed that the longcase clock that stood in the back seemed to be working, even though the time wasn't accurate. It was about five minutes behind."

"I wonder whether, on the hour, it would start announcing it? In the middle of an aria?" Isla commented. "Alas, they moved it away for the next scene, so we shall never know." Isla fanned herself. "My word, it is hot in here."

Teddy immediately jumped to attention. "Let me acquire some refreshments, then."

Isla and Catherine continued chatting about the opera when Catherine interrupted herself and waved to a lady on the other side of the auditorium. "There is Lady Cressy. She must have returned from Bath." She looked at Isla with some hesitation. "I would dearly like to go speak to her, but it would be cumbersome for her to make her way here. Would you mind if I went to her? You could join me, even."

"I shall wait here, for if Teddy returns with the refreshments and finds us gone, he will be rather put out."

"Then at least draw the curtains at the front of the box so that the entire theatre doesn't become aware that you are on your own and that I am a terrible chaperone for having shamefully deserted you." She pulled the heavy scarlet curtains closed to shield Isla from curious stares. Isla waved her away, and Catherine left, leaving Isla sitting alone in the box.

She sat down and pulled out her fan. It was intolerably stifling.

She heard the door behind her open and was glad that Teddy had finally returned with a glass of refreshing drink. "That was faster than expected."

She was about to turn around when a voice, eerily familiar, hissed, "Do not turn around." Isla froze. "Do not turn around," the voice repeated, low and edged with ice.

She would recognise it anywhere. Hard as steel, sharp as a blade—the voice from the gambling club.

Lucian Night. In her opera box.

Her heart leapt into her throat, hammering wildly. Her fingers clenched around the edge of her chair as she forced herself to keep staring ahead at the closed curtain.

Her tongue darted out to wet her lips. "This is a rather risky place for a rendezvous." She attempted flippancy, but the breathlessness in her voice betrayed her.

"I did say I would contact you whenever and wherever I deemed fit. The moment is now." She jolted at the nearness of his voice, which was far closer than she had expected. Impossibly close. His presence pressed in around her, the heat of him at her back. A shiver ghosted over her skin. She could hear him breathe. All it would take was one quick turn, a single wild impulse, and she would see him. She could yank the curtain aside and reveal him to the whole theatre—

"Do not dare to think of it," he whispered. "If you turn, you will lose more than you could possibly have bargained for."

She sucked in a sharp breath. "How did you know—"

"Your brother is my warranty." A threat. Clear and unmistakable.

"What do you mean?" Isla demanded, alarm sharpening her voice.

"Simply that. If you misbehave, your brother will feel the repercussions."

Her grip tightened on the armrest. "Leave my brother out of this. This is between you and me. He need not know anything about this, nor should you use him as leverage."

Lucian chuckled, a slow, mocking sound. "My dear," he drawled, his voice turning oily, "things are never as simple as that. My reach extends far and wide, and your brother, well... How shall I put it?" He paused, as if savouring the moment. "Arch-nemesis seems a fitting term. I have a score to settle with him, and thanks to you, I hold the advantage."

A feeling of foreboding settled over Isla. "What do you mean?"

"Only that his own sister has willingly placed herself in my hands. A fascinating turn of events, wouldn't you say?"

A cold, clammy hand clenched itself over Isla's stomach. "You'd never," she stammered.

He leaned over and whispered into her ear. "I could simply kidnap you, you know. Here and now."

She felt how his warm breath brushed her ears, her neck and stirred her hair. She sucked in a sharp breath.

"Of course, I will take advantage of it. Otherwise, I wouldn't live up to my name as the Lord of the Underworld."

An ice-cold stab of fear flashed through Isla. She'd been naïve and foolish, and she'd made a terrible mistake. Of course, she should have thought of this earlier. Why hadn't she? Had she honestly believed it would be possible to deal with Lucian Night as a real business partner? Had she truly believed it would be as easy as that? If anything ever happened to Algie, she would never forgive herself.

"I retract my request." Her voice sounded wooden. "Forget the entire thing. Since we have no contract and since I never signed anything, I don't owe you anything."

"Ah, my dear, things are not as simple as that." He'd leaned back a bit, and Isla was relieved not to have to feel his breath against her neck anymore.

"It is. I have decided I no longer need your help."

"Very well," he said smoothly. "What do you want me to tell your erstwhile lover, then?"

Isla would have whirled around then, if an iron hand hadn't clamped itself on her shoulder to freeze her into her place.

"Do not turn around," he hissed.

"Who do you mean?" Isla's mouth had gone dry. "Surely, you don't mean—"

"Jem Fawe. We found him. It was rather easier than we'd thought it would be. But I gather since you have changed your mind about him, you no longer need my services. You'll still have to pay for them, though."

Isla's pulse skittered. "Jem. You found Jem? Truly?"

"Ah. It appears the lady might have changed her mind again." The sound of wood scraping on the floor indicated that he was pulling a chair closer behind her. She heard him sit.

"I gather we are to resume our arrangement?"

"I want to meet Jem."

"Very well. But the conditions still stand."

Isla jerked in her chair. She'd entirely forgotten about them. "Truly, you must have been joking. Surely you merely uttered those ridiculous demands to shock me," she started hotly.

"Not entirely," he replied lazily. "I was perfectly serious."

Isla shook her head. "I never signed anything."

"It is no matter, since we don't conduct business in the usual manner."

"Wha-what do you mean?"

"Simply that: if you do not keep your side of the bargain, I shall have to resort to more stringent methods." He leaned forward, and once more she felt his breath on her neck. "Applying some pressure on your brother."

Isla bit on her lips. She'd got herself into a veritable pickle. On the other hand: Jem! If he'd truly found Jem... after all these years... She felt a hot knot of tears rise in her throat. She swallowed it away, and when she could trust her voice again, replied: "Very well. But first I need to verify whether it is truly Jem you found. I don't trust you. You could take anyone and hire them and tell them to pass as Jem Fawe."

"After all this time, would you recognise him, truly?" His voice sounded curious.

Isla was certain she would. "Always."

"Very well then, Lady Isla. Why don't you see for yourself whether it is your man we have? At the Angel Inn tomorrow afternoon. Jem Fawe will be waiting for you there."

She heard him stand. "If it is not him, our agreement is null and void. If, however, it is him..." He bent forward and his lips nearly touched her neck. Her entire body broke out in goosebumps and every single hair on her body stood on end. She heard a rushing in her ears. "I could take my first here and now." His hot breath moved up and down her neck, his lips not quite touching her skin. Isla froze to a salt statue, with only her chest heaving. "But no." He stood up, and she nearly collapsed in relief. "Delayed pleasure is always the best."

She heard footsteps, and the air rushed into the box as the door opened and closed. She did not care. She jumped up, turned, stormed to the door, and was confronted with a crowd of people into which he must have melted like butter into soup. It was impossible to tell who he was. More likely, he was long gone.

Dizziness took hold of her and she clutched the door for support.

"Isla!" Teddy arrived with a footman in tow who carried a silver tray with drinks. "Are you well? You look somewhat pale."

"I—I am fine. I am just hot and thirsty." She took the champagne glass that he held out thankfully, drank it all down in one gulp, and requested another glass. She would get drunk if she did that, but at the moment, she did not care.

"Dreadful crush," Teddy said. "I was lucky to find this fellow to help with the drinks. To navigate a tray with glasses and bottles through this crowd is quite a feat." He pressed a generous tip into his hand and sent him out of the box. "But where is Lady Redgrave?"

"She left to greet a friend. She'll be back in a moment." As soon as she'd said that, the door opened, and Catherine entered.

"Ah, drinks, just what I need." She picked up a glass and drank it as thirstily as Isla had done. The gong that announced the second act sounded, requesting the audience to return to their seats.

"I must say, I am enjoying myself," Catherine told Teddy, "and I am looking forward to this second act."

But Isla's concentration was gone, and she hardly took in anything that happened on stage.

Tomorrow.

The Angel Inn.

She would see Jem again.

After twenty years.

Chapter Nine

THE ANGEL WAS an infamous public house located on St Giles High Street.

Highwaymen and other criminals, imprisoned in Newgate, traditionally stopped there for their last drink before they were executed at Tyburn Tree. They were usually followed by a horde of onlookers, and the atmosphere tended to be one of overall excitement, as though this were a village fair, not an execution. Or so they said.

Isla descended from the carriage and lifted her head to study the seedy, run-down building. Did Lucian Night stop here, too, for his final drink, before he went to his disastrous execution? A cold shiver ran down her spine. She pulled her shawl closer. She stepped aside as a coach pulled up next to her, spattering her with mud. The Angel was also a coaching inn, but certainly not one of the reputable sort. The Quality, certainly, would never dream of stopping there. They would frequent the more expensive coaching inns away from St Giles, such as the

Golden Rooster. And if they had to make a stop here, they would never deign to descend and enter the inn but wait in the carriage, whilst the drinks were brought out to them. Isla regarded the inn with trepidation. Should she really set foot inside it?

"This looks like a perfectly fine place to have some tea." Teddy stepped up to her, offering his arm.

She'd brought along Teddy again. Teddy, who had no clue what was going on. Teddy, who thought they were on another excursion to pass the day. He'd spent the entire coach ride talking about his favourite horologist, Thomas Tompion. She knew a lot more about this seventeenth-century horologist than she cared for. Interestingly, though, she had not found his discourse boring or pedantic, and welcomed the distraction; otherwise, she'd be worrying herself into a state regarding the upcoming meeting. But Teddy distracted her beautifully. The passion in his voice, the sparkle in his eyes and his overall lively demeanour as he discussed his favourite topic had awakened an interest in her as well. She watched his animated face during the entire ride to St Giles.

"Imagine that, Lala—" Her heart warmed when he used the nickname, which he did more and more often. "Tompion's longcase clock from 1680 and a double-pull table clock are still functioning to this very day! What they produce nowadays cannot compare." He pulled out a pocket watch. "Do you see this? I bought it on Bond Street the other day, thinking it must be of good quality. But look, the timing is already incorrect, even though it ran perfectly well in the shop." He flipped the case shut.

"My plan is to take it apart and to fix it and put it together again." He looked at her with a boyish smile.

"How many hours do you spend taking clocks apart and putting them together again?" Isla had asked, regarding the timepiece in his hands.

"Maybe five, no, six hours. The first thing I do after I rise, and even before breakfast, is go to my workshop. Did I tell you about my workshop? I have transformed one room dedicated specifically to clockwork." He described in detail what the room looked like. Then he interrupted himself and looked at her, shyly. "I would love to have a workshop in our new home as well."

Isla blinked. "By all means. Of course, you shall have as many workshops as you like, and you can mount as many clocks as you want on the walls." Though she privately thought that the incessant ticking would, in all likelihood, drive her to insanity.

"Thank you for indulging my eccentricities," he said. "I know my interests are unusual and they have elicited many comments from certain persons. Currently, it is more fashionable to be interested in poetry, or painting nature; botany, geology and biology are all perfectly fine interests for a gentleman to have these days, but not the mechanics of man-made machines, such as clocks. They are said to lack emotion and romance. Though I say with a certain amount of conviction that machines and engines are our future."

"You shouldn't mind so much what other people say about your eccentricities, as you call them," Isla retorted. "I am the least person to object to them, having so many of my own. After all, here you are again accompanying me on one of my strange excursions. You must think I must have fallen in love with this terrible part of town." She indicated with a hand outside the carriage window, where they passed the worst part of the rookery.

"Not so strange at all," Teddy retorted eagerly. "I have heard of your charities, for it is well known that Lady Isla is one of the biggest benefactresses in town. You not only support hospitals but orphanages, and I had heard of your ventures into the less reputable parts of town to save the lost souls long before we even met." It was true, for Isla had, in the past, liked to seek out the less fortunate to provide help and support. She knew what it was like to be homeless. To be an orphan. To be uprooted and not to know where one belonged. To be driven to do what one had to do to survive, even if it meant lying and stealing. Teddy would never know, but she herself had once stolen handkerchiefs, timepieces and purses. Together with Jem.

Her eyes shifted back to the sombre building in front of her. The Angel. What an ironic name. She turned to Teddy, suddenly having made up her mind to tell him the truth. "This is no charitable visit. I am here to meet someone. An acquaintance from long ago. A man. A childhood friend, to be precise. We haven't seen each other for over twenty years. I asked Lucian Night to help me find him." The latter she hadn't exactly planned on telling him, but there it was. The words had tumbled out of her mouth.

He regarded her calmly. "Let us meet the fellow, then."

She returned his regard. "You don't mind at all that your betrothed has sought out the worst criminal in the

London underworld to help her find her old friend. Whom we are about to meet right now."

Teddy scratched the back of his neck. "To be sure, it is somewhat irregular. But I must admit I'm rather curious now what the fellow looks like. And," a grin stole across his lips, "I confess I crave a good, strong cup of tea."

THE ANGEL inside was exactly as she'd expected it would be. Dark and dingy, with suspicious-looking characters skulking in every corner. Isla paused nervously by the entrance, but Teddy strode right into the room like it was the most natural thing in the world and as though he were accustomed to frequenting places like this.

Did Isla imagine it, or did a hush settle over the room when they entered? She felt the stares of a hundred pairs of eyes on her like pinpricks. There were probably only a dozen or so people in the room; quite possibly fewer. The innkeeper, a fat, bald man with a greasy apron, stepped forward from behind the bar and eyed them with small, beady eyes. He sized them up and recognised them for Quality.

Isla wished she'd not put on her best velvet walking dress, nor her fine new bonnet; this, together with the reticule and umbrella in her hand, surely gave her away for who she was: a lady of Quality. But for some reason, she'd wanted to look her best when she finally met Jem.

After her eyes adjusted to the darkness of the room, Isla's gaze swept across it, but it appeared Jem wasn't there yet. She was momentarily relieved. She'd agonised the entire morning over what to wear, and she'd changed clothes three, four times until she'd settled on the current ensemble. Now she wished she'd chosen a simpler dress, a less elaborate redingote, for the one she was wearing now was of dark green velvet with golden frogging in a criss-cross pattern in the military style that was so fashionable these days. It made her look expensive.

Isla stepped close to Teddy, who lifted his hand with his walking stick, hailing the innkeeper as if they were old friends.

The innkeeper paused and stared. "We'd like a table somewhere private, somewhere that isn't in a dark and draughty corner." Teddy looked around. "Preferably somewhere where people don't blow the smoke of their pipes into our faces, either. By the window or the fireplace would be best." But alas, these tables were occupied. There was an elderly man sitting by the window; a group of men were next to him, apparently drunk and playing dice. Isla was too nervous to register what happened next, but the innkeeper, who'd leered at them only a moment before, froze, jerked and stood to attention, and made a movement with his hand that Isla couldn't interpret. As if on command, everyone at the tables got up and left. Isla and Teddy were the only ones remaining in the room, save for the innkeeper, who bowed.

"What happened?" Isla whispered to Teddy, looking around in confusion. "Why did everyone leave?"

Teddy shrugged. "I said we needed privacy, so I suppose that is what we got." He lowered his voice. "Very obliging of him, don't you think?"

The innkeeper was behaving oddly, but Isla could not focus enough to wonder why. She sat at the table, tugged off her gloves, and kept surveying the room, which was entirely empty. Teddy took his place across from her. Isla wondered whether it had been a mistake to take him along, whether she should tell him to sit elsewhere. What if Jem was intimidated by his presence?

As soon as she thought that, she nearly laughed, for Teddy was the least intimidating person in the entire universe. He was now conversing with the innkeeper about what beverage to order.

"What would you like?" he asked her. "Just regular tea or something more fortifying?"

"Just tea, please."

"For me as well," Teddy told the innkeeper.

"Certainly, right away." The innkeeper bowed so low that she had a clear view of his bald head.

"It's somewhat of an odd place," Teddy commented as he took off his top hat and set it aside. "Though the service seems to be good."

The innkeeper promptly served a pot of piping hot tea that was so strong, Isla nearly gagged. She added two, three lumps of sugar and a good dollop of milk and stirred, her eyes incessantly scanning the room. Her forehead puckered into a worried frown as her mind went wild with possible scenarios. Had Lucian Night deceived her? Was this a hoax? Maybe Jem would never appear. It could be a scheme to entrap them, to kidnap them, to ask for ransom money from Algie. Worry churned in her stomach.

"Let us finish the tea and leave," she told Teddy. "It

doesn't look like Jem is about to appear any time soon, and I have a strange feeling about this place. It doesn't seem safe."

"It does seem to be a seedy place. Do you think it is a hotbed of criminals? The innkeeper appears to be reasonable enough."

"It is possible. We're in St Giles, after all."

"Never fear, Lala. If something happens, I shall do my best to defend you. I have some skill at boxing, even though I was knocked out immediately after the first few minutes during my last practice."

He touched his chin, wincing, as if still remembering the punch. "Besides, I have my stick." He lifted it. "It can serve as a weapon."

A ghost of a smile appeared on Isla's face. "And I have my umbrella. At least it has a deadly point. I really should ask Algie to give me lessons in shooting. He's one of the best shots in the entire country."

"Is he, really? Why haven't you done so, yet?"

She pulled a face. "I don't care much for the loud noise. And the smell." She shuddered.

"Sulphur and saltpetre from the powder that gets ignited." Teddy pushed up his spectacles. "A sharp, acrid smell. Together with some smoke."

"I wish they hadn't invented it. Our world would be a better place." Even thinking of the smell evoked an image of her lying under a carriage, surrounded by the harsh, metallic scent of burnt gunpowder, smoke and fire. There had been a sudden, deafening bang, and she'd found herself flung through the carriage. The world toppled and turned...and when she'd awoken again, a soft hand was bathing her forehead. Vanya.

"...if you imagine that gunpowder was invented as far back as the Tang Dynasty in China," Teddy was saying.

Isla jerked back to attention. She was about to tell him to repeat what he'd said, when suddenly the door opened, bringing with it a welcome blast of fresh, cold air.

A tall, lanky man had entered. Dark, long hair hung over his forehead and curled at his nape. He wore loose trousers stuffed into boots, a shirt and waistcoat with big, shiny buttons, a hat at a rakish angle, and a bandanna about his neck. He had a moustache twirling over his upper lip. Isla's words remained stuck in her throat as she stared. The man swaggered into the room, hailed the innkeeper, and sat down at a table in a corner on the other side of the room. His eyes swept the room, took her in, and paused at her companion. Then he seemed to dismiss them as he hailed the innkeeper for a mug of ale.

Teddy looked at him, fascinated. "I suppose this is our fellow?"

Isla rose. "If you'll excuse me?"

Isla had never been so nervous in her entire life as she crossed the room from one side to the other. Her heart slammed against her ribcage, and her knees were weak. It was a miracle she could walk. Her eyes bored into the man, who lifted his mug to take a deep, long draught of ale. Was he truly Jem? How could one correctly identify a person one had known twenty years earlier as a child? The hair colour was correct. Little Jem's hair, too, had been dark and long, and had curled at his nape. She could not know about his height, but she supposed Jem would have been tall and lean, like the man before her. The dress was correct; it was that of the people of the Rom. His linen shirt was colourfully embroidered with red and blue thread, something which Vanya had liked to do. Red for strength, she'd said, and blue for protection. The patterns were spirals and horseshoes, both symbols for luck.

As she approached, she saw the frays at his sleeves, the baggy boots and the threadbare trousers. His face was narrow, his forehead and nose proud, the cheekbones high, his chin square.

It could, indeed, be Jem. An adult version of him. As he lifted the mug, she saw that his wrist was strong and tanned, as if from outside labour. He wore a bracelet around his wrist, one that had been made of red and blue strings.

"Jem Fawe." She stood in front of his table.

He stared at her, equally incredulous as she must have looked. His gaze travelled down her figure, taking in her expensive dress, her bonnet, her shawl, her reticule.

"Isla?"

Chapter Ten

Isla's knees finally gave way, and she collapsed in the chair across from him.

"Jem. Is it really you?" She spoke in Romani.

He set down his mug, a look of incredulity on his face. "You still speak our language?"

She nodded. "Of course."

"You've turned into a lady." He shook his head.

Isla fiddled with the cord of her reticule. "Yes. Well. What else might I have become?"

"I meant, of course, a fine lady." He cleared his throat. "A toff." His eyes pierced hers. "But then we knew that your father was a marquess, and that you were taken in by the Quality." Somehow it sounded like a reprimand.

"Yes." She searched his face for a hint of recrimination or judgment, but it was neutral. He lifted his mug again, drank, and set it down.

A slight feeling of ill-ease assailed her.

Was this truly her Jem? Jem, who'd been her heart and her soul.

The person sitting in front of her was a stranger. Indifferent. Detached. As if none of their shared memories mattered. As if they had never happened. Not anymore. Not now that she'd joined the *gadje* and become a 'toff'.

Isla shivered. *Where do we even begin?*

"How have you fared?" she asked at last.

"Good." He shrugged one shoulder. "Well enough."

A pause. Twenty years of silence stretched between them.

"What happened after I left?"

"I ran away." He took a swig of his ale. "London, to be precise."

Isla searched his face anxiously. A thirteen-year-old boy, alone in London. A Gypsy, orphaned, and not a penny to his name. There was only one thing such a boy could do. She shifted uneasily in her chair.

"And then?"

He shrugged again. "Lasted a fortnight before they threw me into Newgate. Got caught pickpocketing a toff on Oxford Street."

Isla gasped.

"Stroke of fortune, that. Met a man there. Mr Berkenwell. A blacksmith, locked up for fraud. But he got out, and he paid to get me released. Took me in as an apprentice. Learned the trade. Kept my hands clean." He spread his hands in front of her, and she noticed he had grime under his fingernails.

Isla let out a shaking breath.

"But once a Gypsy, always a Gypsy." A wry smile tugged at his lips. "Restlessness is in our blood, you know. After a while, I left the forge and went back to my roots." He leaned back. "I'm in the horse trade now. More lucrative, too."

She met his gaze. "I'm glad." She wanted to ask so much more. Things like: *If you were in London, why did you never look for me? Why did you never come to our meeting spot? I should have been easy to find...* and: *What happened to you that you became so...indifferent?*

Maybe it was Newgate. Or life that had hardened him. Maybe his brush with the criminal world had been greater than he'd let on. For there was a toughness encasing him, a sharp-eyed, calculating shrewdness in his eyes, even as he sized her up. It wasn't the glance that a friend would give to his long-lost friend, as they finally reunited.

Maybe he wasn't Jem, after all.

She almost wished he wasn't.

But all these doubts were cast into the wind with his next words.

"And you, *lelori*?" A little smile played about his lips. "I see life has treated you well."

Isla gasped. "You do remember. You used to call me that." Only Jem had ever called her that. It had been his secret pet name for her.

"'Course I remember." He leaned back lazily, and there was a mocking glint in his eyes. "I remember everything. My little *lelori*. We were quite a pair. You used to sing and dance with Vanya while I collected the coins." He smirked. "Not only from my tin box."

A steep frown appeared on Isla's forehead. "What do you mean?"

"You know. While a toff will throw in a meagre half farthing, there's so much more to be had from his plump pockets, if you have the finger for it." He grinned and twirled a coin between his knuckles. He sounded almost proud.

She looked at him with a furrowed brow. Since when was Jem proud of stealing? "But Vanya said—"

Vanya had given Jem the thrashing of a lifetime when she'd caught him pickpocketing. "This is what gives the rest of us a bad name," she'd scolded. "You make an honest living using your own hands, through whatever means possible. You do not steal. Ever."

Maybe Jem was referring to that first time, during a performance, when Vanya had caught him. Isla didn't know how often he'd done it after that. She knew he'd done so, secretly, never admitting to it. For they had been hungry, and Vanya's rules had often come second to survival.

Yes, that was what he must mean.

Isla's brow cleared.

"Everything in this world revolves around blunt," Jem continued. "You got some? Life is sweet. You got none? You must see how you go about getting some using whatever means possible. That's all life is."

"Yes, well, I think things are slightly more complicated than that."

He crossed his arms behind his head and leaned back in his chair. "It's because our world is divided into the haves and the have-nots. Call it karma. Call it fate. The will of God. Whatever. You," he nodded at her, "have brazenly crossed the line back and forth between the haves and the have-nots, only to return to the haves, where you were born after all."

Isla nodded.

"But the rest of us ain't so lucky." He uncrossed his arms, rested his elbows on the table, and leaned forward, his eyes gleaming. "We ain't so lucky at all. It would seem only right that the haves would help the have-nots. Don't you think so?"

She looked at him in confusion for one moment, before the penny dropped.

He was asking her for money.

"Oh." Her fingers cramped over her reticule. Her purse was inside with her pocket money. She opened it with shaking fingers and shook the contents out on the table.

A purse with some coins, an enamelled flask with hartshorn salt, a silken handkerchief, and the pocket watch that Teddy had given her.

He studied the items with interest.

She picked up the purse, which was plump. Rather than shaking the coins out on the table and counting them, she shoved it across the table towards Jem, without meeting his eyes. "Here, take it."

He took it, opened it, peeked inside, smiled, and bowed. "My lady."

"You can also have the flask."

But he'd picked up the pocket watch and was regarding it with interest.

"Not this. It was given to me by, by—" Teddy!

Teddy was here, and she'd forgotten about him entirely. She turned, and there he was, at the table in the corner, patiently drinking his third cup of tea.

A feeling of such relief swept over her, she felt almost dizzy.

She turned back to Jem, more resolute. "You can have the flask and the handkerchief. It is real silk, but you can't have my pocket watch. My betrothed gave it to me. In fact, he is here with us."

Jem cast a glance in the corner, placed it back on the table and shoved it back to her. "Ah, of course, if it's a present from your future husband, then I'll not touch it."

But he swept up the other items, and they disappeared into his pockets before she could blink.

Teddy must have seen them glance in his direction. He got up, dusted his trousers off, and came over to their table.

"There he is, the husband," Jem said with a vague smirk.

"Teddy." Isla looked up at him, glad that he was here. "This is Jem Fawe. Jem, this is Lord Thaddaeus Linwood."

The two men eyed each other with open curiosity.

"Please. Don't let me disrupt your conversation. I see you have much to catch up on," Teddy said easily.

"I think we are done," Isla said, getting up. She held out her hand to Jem. "It was... good to see you again, Jem. After all this time." She searched for more words but couldn't, for the life of her, think of anything else to say.

He took her hand and bowed over it with a flourishing movement. "Lady Isla," he said in a mocking tone. "It was a pleasure."

Teddy helped Isla into the carriage. She leaned back and closed her eyes.

"Interesting sort of fellow," Teddy observed as the carriage set in motion. "The pattern on his shirt was most interesting. Seems to have something to do with horses."

"He is a horse trainer," Isla said.

"Ah. I heard that many Gypsies have this occupation. Seems suitable. I confess I have little skill when it comes to horses. The creatures keep wanting to bite me whenever I get too close."

Isla didn't answer.

"I do invariably better with machines than with animals." He paused. "Isla?"

Then she burst into tears.

And it wasn't the delicate, ladylike kind of weeping, either, but loud, messy sobbing, with nose running, breath hitching, and all.

Teddy looked utterly at a loss. Most gentlemen were, when faced with a crying woman. They never quite knew what to do. Ignore it? Offer a handkerchief? Pat her shoulder awkwardly and murmur something soothing?

Whatever they chose to do, it was nearly always the wrong thing, adding a fresh layer of misery to the one already in tears.

But Teddy, thankfully, did the right thing.

He switched to her side of the seat, moved closer to her, so that his shoulder almost touched hers, gently nudging her. And Isla understood. He was offering his shoulder.

She turned toward him and buried her face in his shoulder.

And wept.

Teddy didn't say anything at all. He did not attempt to console her through words, nor did he ignore her sadness.

Instead, he pulled out a handkerchief and handed it to her quietly.

Isla took it and blew into it loudly.

"I beg your pardon," she said in a wavering voice. "I don't know what has come over me."

"I suppose one cannot help but get rather emotional when one is suddenly confronted with a childhood friend one hasn't seen for over twenty years," Teddy commented. "It is completely understandable. If I were in your shoes, I would probably do the same. In fact," he added after a short pause, "I feel like bawling right along with you out of mere sympathy. I think I need the hand-kerchief back, if you please."

That remark elicited a watery laugh from Isla, so that she found herself crying and laughing at the same time.

"I'm afraid I made your shoulder all wet." She dabbed at it with her handkerchief.

After she'd thoroughly dried her face and blown her nose, and felt more composed, Teddy asked carefully, "So I gather he wasn't who you expected?"

Isla sighed. "I don't know what I expected." She pondered on her words, only to retract them. "I suppose that's not true. The harsh truth is that he didn't come up to my expectations." She looked at him with troubled eyes. "Is that so terrible of me?"

"In what sense didn't he meet your expectations?"

Once more, Isla had to ponder over this. "He was no longer the Jem I used to know." A deep sadness filled her. "I suppose that is only natural, as we knew each other when we were children, and even though we had a close bond, it would be naïve to expect a person to remain unchanged, both physically as well as character-wise, as they grow up. I made that mistake: I expected him to stay the same."

But even as she uttered those words, she realised they were not the truth. What she had really hoped, deep down, was that their connection had remained the same; with the same sincere, child-like trust and light-hearted friendship and outlook on life.

Even though he'd felt familiar—his appearance, the way he spoke, some gestures, even—she hadn't felt any friendship towards the Jem Fawe she'd met. There had been a chasm between them, as deep as the gorge Dante wrote about in his *Inferno*. They were strangers to each other.

And yes, even when he called her by the endearment that was reserved only for her, she had been glad that he'd remembered, but she hadn't felt any closer to him.

And that was why she'd cried.

She'd mourned the loss of a friendship that she'd hung on to all her life, ever since she'd been a little girl.

As the carriage pulled up in front of Algie's town house, Teddy hesitated before descending. "I think you need some time alone this evening. Shall we postpone tonight's theatre visit? Shakespeare will not go away, and Hamlet will be there tomorrow."

Isla looked at him thankfully. "Thank you for understanding. You have been an invaluable support today." She pressed his hand.

Teddy looked at her warmly. "Always." He did not release her hand. "There is something I want you to know, Lala."

She looked at him inquisitively.

He drew in a deep breath. "I love you, Lala. More than I can properly express."

Isla froze.

"I just need you to know that."

Isla searched for words. "I—I—I don't know what to say." Something told her that that was probably not what he'd hoped she'd say at that moment, but her mind had momentarily shut down with emotion. It was simply too much. First Jem, with his entire lack of emotion, now Teddy, who exhibited too much.

She drew a shaking hand over her brow.

Teddy nodded. "I know. You need not say anything at all." He released her hand gently.

She turned towards the townhouse, but shortly before she reached the door, she turned to him. "I am very fond of you," she said in a low voice, so low that he had to bend down to understand her. "But..." She searched for words. "You must give me time."

Chapter Eleven

Isla found Algie in his study, in his leather chair in front of the fire, as always, peeling oranges as he went through the dispatches of the day.

He looked up and, at a glance, saw that something was the matter. He set the orange aside.

"So, the fellow you met at the Angel wasn't who you expected him to be," he concluded.

Isla stumbled. Trust Algie to always startle her in the most unexpected moments.

She furrowed her brow. "How did you know I went to the Angel Inn?" She'd taken such care not to use any of Algie's carriages, none of his retainers had accompanied them, and she'd not breathed a word to Algie about her exploits.

"My dear." He folded his hands over his stomach and looked at her in a self-satisfied way. "You should know by now that I know everything."

"Yes. But, how? Which of your spies did you send after me this time? Or wasn't that necessary? Wait." She placed a finger on her nose as she thought. "You have informers at the inn." Only one other person had been there with her and Teddy. Her eyes widened. "The innkeeper? That scoundrel!"

Algie chuckled. "I shan't reveal that. But rest assured, I have my sources. Why do you think I allow you to scamper off into the most scandalous areas of London? Because I know you are safely surrounded by my men. Of course, my informers always keep you, and that Linwood fellow, within their sights."

Isla settled on the ground beside his armchair and felt foolish. Of course. She should have known that. She'd always thought her brother's lack of concern to be a tad unnatural every time she'd scampered off into the rookery. He had no reason to worry since he'd had her shadowed by his men.

"You won't have to do that anymore. Your informers will find themselves twiddling their thumbs in the future. I have decided not to visit the rookery anymore." She paused before continuing. "Not even for charity purposes."

She would never set foot in St Giles, or the Angel, or any of those places ever again.

Algie looked at her, and a glimmer of sympathy flickered through his watery, pale blue eyes. "That bad?"

She felt a lump rise in her throat, and she swallowed bravely before retorting. "I am merely disappointed, that is all."

"Tell me about it."

She did.

Algie frowned. "That is a shame. But I suppose it was

inevitable. Life has hardened him. And as you know better than most, life among the Rom is never easy. I do sympathise with their plight, truly. But as you also know, there is little appetite in the House of Lords for more lenient legislation. Society's prejudice against the Romani runs far too deep. The time simply hasn't come."

Isla agreed with a sigh.

"If you consider what he must have gone through, everything which he hasn't told you, it is understandable that he would no longer be the same person. He is no longer the Jem you remember. That boy is long gone."

Isla lowered her head, for he'd spoken the truth. "It was important for me to see him, even if realising that he was not the boy I had enshrined in my memory all these years. It was that glorification of a memory that kept me going." Her shoulders slumped. "How very silly of me."

"Maybe not." He patted her hands. "You'd make an excellent agent for my office, with your ability to find people." He proceeded to stuff his pipe.

Isla looked at him, her eyes growing into big, round saucers, as something else dawned on her. "Algie. Never say. Never say you knew that I met—Lucian Night."

The expression on his face spoke volumes.

"Of course I knew," he said, as he lit his pipe.

Isla fell back on her heels, stunned. "But I don't understand. You said you had a devil of a time finding Night. And there I was, finding him without any problems."

"I never said I couldn't find him. I said it was difficult to arrest him. There is a difference." He stuck the pipe into a corner of his mouth.

Isla digested that.

"Besides, it isn't entirely disadvantageous for him to still be free and to attract the attention of the Mudlark Skulls, who are currently wreaking havoc on the Thames, and are thereby in direct conflict with Night, for they have encroached on his territory. We can catch two flies with one swat if we play them out against each other."

The butler arrived with more dispatches, and that was the sign for Isla to remove herself. She got up from the floor, shook out her skirts and said, "I'll leave you to your work."

Chapter Twelve

THE NEXT MORNING, Teddy was waiting excitedly in the hallway with news: he had finally found a house that would suit them. "And the best thing is, there is an additional room in the basement that one could transform into a workshop..."

Isla listened to him patiently, fiddling with the string of her reticule. She felt awkward in his presence after he'd so effusively confessed his feelings, and she knew she hadn't responded as he deserved. But what did she feel?

It was true what she'd said that she felt fond of him. More than fond. Protective, almost like a mother hen felt protective toward one of her chicks.

Isla looked at him with a start. Did she truly just compare Teddy to a cuddly little yellow chick? True, he wasn't exactly tall, but for her diminutive size, he was tall enough. He was stocky and sturdy and, as she'd discovered, rather muscular under his tailored coats. The results of his time spent boxing, no doubt.

She somehow found him slightly better looking than

before, too. Whereas previously she'd found his appearance to be hardly memorable, if not bland, she now found that she no longer thought so. While not exactly handsome, he had a pleasant enough appearance. There was something charming about those spectacles that kept sliding down his nose, and his innocent, chocolate brown eyes, and his incessant talk about horology.

As Isla studied him, he somehow veered from the subject of their town house to the clock on St George's Church, which was nearby, commenting that the clock was off by a minute, and that that would no doubt irritate him every time they passed it, which was the only negative aspect of living so close to that church.

"On the positive side, I enjoy hearing the bells," he concluded, looking at Isla expectantly.

"Yes. Well, let us have a look at the house," she replied.

He was right. It was a pretty, white stuccoed terraced house with two elegant Corinthian pillars framing the entrance. Sunlight flooded through the tall, arched windows that faced Maddox Street.

"Will it do?" He looked at Isla expectantly.

She smiled. "I think it will do very well."

OVER THE COMING DAYS, Isla found herself busy shopping for her trousseau. Together with Catherine, they frequented haberdasheries, milliners, cordwainers, and hosiery shops. Shopping was a welcome distraction, and Isla found she was able to put the events of the past few days behind her.

Teddy, too, increased his attentiveness and took her to the Amphitheatre, the Royal Menagerie, and the Egyptian Exhibit.

Tonight, they would spend an evening at Vauxhall. Catherine would join them, and, to everyone's surprise, Algie announced that he would accompany them as well.

Arriving in a boat, they saw a million little lights twinkling from the Chinese lampions that hung from the trees. Strains of music hovered in the air, and there was a general atmosphere of gaiety and delight.

"The last time we were here you bought me a bag of comfits, sugared almonds, I believe, which I enjoyed very much," Isla said, turning to Algie, who'd been sitting mutely beside her during the entire boat ride. It seemed that shyness had taken hold of him again now that he was in the presence of Catherine, who was sitting next to Teddy, chattering away.

"Did I?" Algie muttered.

"Yes. And then there was such a squeeze as a balloon was about to ascend, and I dropped the bag on the ground."

"Now I remember. You crawled about on all fours to gather the sweets again, but we didn't see that. We thought you'd suddenly disappeared and searched the entire premises for you." Algie shook his head. "Just don't repeat that, if you please. Don't simply disappear like that."

At those words, Teddy looked at them curiously. "Why would she disappear?" he asked. "For as long as you are with me, there is no possibility of that happening."

Algie snorted but did not deign to retort.

The relationship between Teddy and Algie seemed to be fraught with complications, Isla noted. Algie did not appear to hold Teddy in very high regard. While he accepted him as his sister's betrothed, he also made it clear that he considered Teddy to be somewhat of a nitwit.

Teddy, in turn, was overly intimidated by Algie to the point that he could merely stutter whenever Algie addressed him directly.

And Algie, of course, spoke not a word, but stared mutely at Catherine, who attempted to chat with all and sundry, including the boatman.

Isla herself had been absent-minded and answered in monosyllables to Teddy's and Catherine's attempts at conversation. Only when the lights of Vauxhall appeared did she snap out of it, as the memories surfaced.

As the boat docked, Teddy got up and extended a hand to help Isla disembark.

Catherine inhaled deeply as a whiff of fragrant lilacs drifted in the air.

"I haven't been here since Fred passed away. No, longer than that. He proposed to me during the fireworks." A whimsical smile passed over her face. "How long ago that was."

Catherine's marriage to Lord Redgrave had not been happy. Isla assumed that was the reason she was in no hurry to remarry, and why Algie's chances of winning her were rather low.

Isla sighed.

Teddy cast her a quizzical look and squeezed her

hand. Isla met his eyes gratefully. Somehow, they did not have to speak. Teddy understood, and Isla was glad that he did.

Algie had a box reserved at the Plaza, and they dined alfresco on a selection of thinly sliced cold meats, lobster, cheese and olives. For pudding, they had custards and strawberry tarts, all washed down with punch and champagne.

Isla watched with mild amusement as Catherine tried to draw Algie into the conversation. To her surprise, he managed to string together several sentences that went beyond his usual monosyllables. But when a few newcomers joined their table, colleagues, evidently, who recognised Algie at once, Isla's surprise deepened. Her tongue-tied brother seemed to transform before her eyes into the confident, eloquent politician. His public persona, so articulate and self-assured, was a stark contrast to the shy, hesitant man she knew in private.

Catherine, too, had noticed. She leaned back in her chair, idly toying with her pearl necklace, and watched him with interest as he entered an animated debate with a gentleman on some political matter.

Teddy, however, had little interest in politics. He shifted restlessly in his chair, casting impatient glances at the ever-growing crowd around their table. Then he leaned in and said quietly, "Shall we step outside? It's becoming rather crowded."

Isla agreed.

She cast a quick glance at Catherine, who seemed entirely absorbed in Algie's debate with Lord Mountbatten.

Then Teddy took her hand with a gentle tug and led her away from the rising clamour and the press of bodies, into the gardens. Past the hedges and winding paths, they went, toward the quieter, shadowed side of Vauxhall.

Isla breathed a sigh of relief. Here, between the hedges, it was darker, as only the main path was lit by lampions, and the air seemed cooler as well. She shivered, and Teddy immediately enquired whether she was cold.

"I left my shawl at the table. So silly of me." She rubbed her arms. These early summer evenings were still cool, and she should have thought to dress more warmly.

"Should we return to fetch it?" he asked.

Isla shook her head. "No. Then we will have to face the crowd again, and right now, it is good to be away from it all."

They had reached a small pavilion, empty but for a single hanging lampion that cast a soft, wavering glow.

For a moment, there was silence. Then came the faint rustle of fabric, and when Isla looked up, she saw Teddy shrugging off his coat. Before she could object, he gently draped it over her shoulders.

"But now you'll be cold," she murmured.

"I won't," he said simply.

He adjusted the collar for her, and as he did, his fingers brushed her jaw. The touch lingered and sent a ripple of delicious sparks through her. She looked up, heart pounding, and for an instant, the world seemed to pause.

His face was half in shadow, his eyes glinting in the dim light. She couldn't help herself. Her hand rose of its own accord and slipped into his hair. It was thick and soft beneath her fingers.

A breath caught in her throat. She knew what she wanted, what she needed. With sudden boldness, she tugged him closer just as his hand cupped her chin, and then their lips met.

At first, it was soft and tentative, as though they were both unsure. But as their hunger for each other deepened, the kiss grew bolder, slow and sweet, then faster, more urgent. His mouth moved over hers, along her jaw, down the graceful line of her throat, to the hollow at its base. She shivered.

He eased her backward until she met the wall of the pavilion, and still he kissed her, again and again, until he abruptly pulled away and stepped back.

"Enough." His voice was hoarse, his breath uneven.

Isla stood frozen, her body alight, her thoughts scattered to the wind. All she could feel was the aching emptiness where his lips had been.

Teddy cleared his throat. "I think I'd better speak to Wynthorpe about moving the wedding forward. Before... before..." He cleared his throat again.

Isla chuckled. "Here, in the middle of Vauxhall?"

He gave her a meaningful look. "Particularly here, in the middle of Vauxhall. What do you think most couples out here are doing? It's rather scandalous, and I vow I didn't think before I brought you into this part of the gardens."

She looked at him happily. "I don't care. I'm happy we came here." She took his hand. "And yes, you should speak to Algie," she added impishly.

Chapter Thirteen

THAT NIGHT, Isla couldn't sleep. Rather than wake Meggie and drag her from her bed, she put on her slippers, wrapped a woollen shawl around her shoulders, and proceeded down the stairs from her bedroom to the kitchen to warm some milk.

She passed Algie's study and noticed a strip of light beneath the door. That was nothing unusual, for Algie preferred to work late into the night, sometimes even until the early morning hours. She would go to the kitchen first and speak with him afterwards, so she continued her way down the stairs, when a voice stopped her short.

"You will do as I say. Enough is enough."

Her hand froze on the banister. She barely held in a gasp.

Precise. Cold. Commanding.

She'd heard that voice only twice before.

She remained where she was, listening breathlessly.

Her brother murmured something in reply, low and indistinct.

"Do not deceive yourself," said the silken, cold voice, cutting like steel. "You know as well as I do that the entire venture is a farce. It is counter-productive and will not yield what you hope for."

Isla sank down onto the stair, her hand trembling on the railing.

"You are well-advised to do as I say or else be responsible for the consequences."

There was a pause, heavy with threat. Her brother's voice came again; softer now, defensive, almost pleading. He was trying to appease him, that much was clear.

And just as clear was the iron grip Lucian Night had on him. Like a fox with its teeth already sunk into the throat of its prey, the so-called Lord of the Underworld held her brother fast. Not with violence, but with something far more damning.

He was blackmailing Algie.

Of that, there could be no doubt.

Night's voice grew louder, indicating that he was approaching the door. Alarmed, Isla leapt to her feet, fleeing up the stairs to the top floor, just in time before the door opened and swift footsteps echoed through the hallway. With a pounding heart, she peeked over the banister to see what he looked like, the feared Lord of the Underworld.

But all she saw was the billowing hem of his black coat before it vanished through the front door.

. . .

WITH HER MIND STILL WHIRRING, Isla closed her bedroom door and leaned against it. What did it mean?

Why was Lucian Night coming and going in their very home, in the dead of the night?

Why was Algie receiving him?

Why had it sounded like they were in some venture—*together*? And that in this unholy partnership, Night invariably held the upper hand.

And what did that say about Algie?

She felt a migraine beginning to stir. Rubbing her temple, she slid to the floor and sat staring ahead.

Algie had lied to her.

Why?

A sudden uneasiness settled over her. Not only for her brother's safety, but because she could no longer understand him.

And she did not wish him to discover that she had overheard everything.

Isla rose, shook out her nightgown, and climbed into bed. The sheets were cold. She shivered.

One thing was clear: she needed to extricate herself from the bargain she'd made with Lucian Night. It had all come to naught.

She'd already given her first kiss to someone else.

A slight smile crept across her lips as she recalled the night at Vauxhall gardens. Her fingers crept up to her lips and a dreamy look softened her eyes.

Teddy.

She'd given her first kiss to him.

How glad she was.

With considerable satisfaction, she snuggled deeply

into the pillow. She had outwitted Night in that regard, at least.

And she would outwit him in the rest.

Tomorrow, she would seek him out and renegotiate their contract.

She would dress up in men's clothes. And she would take Catherine along, this time, instead of Teddy.

Yes. That was a good plan.

Isla kept her disguise hidden in a chest with a false bottom in a little-used service room in the half-basement. The room, filled with discarded furniture and a narrow bed for visiting servants, was seldom entered. Only Meggie knew of the hiding place.

Isla had discovered it was far safer to change there than to sneak through the entire house in disguise, risking an encounter with one of the servants, or heaven forbid, Algie. After Isla had changed, Meggie would ensure that she could slip out unseen through the servants' entrance. Meggie then would slip out herself and help Isla summon a hackney.

Now, while Meggie kept the cook and the scullery maid occupied, Isla flitted down the corridor and into the service room. She retrieved her clothes from the chest and stepped behind a paravent—a big, ornate screen Algie's father had once brought back from China. Its lacquer was peeling, and the bamboo frame cracked, which was why it had been banished to this forgotten corner.

Fortunately, its placement not only shielded her as

she changed but also concealed the chest. She folded her gown neatly and returned it to its hiding place. Just as she lowered the lid, the door opened and clicked softly shut.

She turned, about to ask Meggie why she wasn't keeping guard, when she heard heavy footsteps on the creaking wooden floor, and the words died on her lips. Those footsteps weren't Meggie's.

These were slower. Heavier.

A rustle. The soft thump of clothing hitting the floor.

Isla held her breath and peeked through a narrow crack on the screen.

It was a man.

She squinted. The light was dim, and no candle had been lit.

The man turned as he shrugged out of his coat, and she saw his profile.

Teddy.

Isla bit her lip hard to keep from making a sound.

What on earth was he doing here?

He was dressed oddly, in a worn suit and hat, like a common labourer.

He loosened his tie and tugged it off, tossing it on top of the coat on the floor.

And then—

Her eyes widened.

He unbuttoned his shirt and let it fall.

Isla had never considered herself easily shocked. Nor was she a prude. She knew all about the male anatomy—she'd had her eyeful when she'd visited the Elgin marbles exhibition. Even Catherine had blushed and averted her eyes when they came upon a Lapith grappling with a centaur, whereas Isla had merely lifted her spectacles and examined the nude male figures with appreciative curiosity.

But this...

How could a mere layer of fabric have concealed *this*?

He was all sinew and rippling muscle, every inch of him honed and powerful. Fascinating, to be sure, but that wasn't what rooted her to the spot.

It was his skin.

Her gaze clung to the intricate images inked over his chest, his arms, and, as he turned, even all over his back. Images of intricate, elaborate detail.

She had read of such things. The Romans had written about ancient Pictish warriors who were covered from head to toe in blue designs. These days, mariners commonly had tattoos. As did soldiers returning from India or the Caribbean.

But Teddy was none of these.

He moved again, stooping to retrieve a clean shirt from a basket near the wall. He turned, and the light of the window fell across his back—and that was when she saw it.

Between his shoulder blades, stark and unmistakable.

A snarling wolf.

The very same image she'd seen on the man she thought she'd stabbed. And in Algie's letter. And on the door in St Giles.

Except this one was larger, sprawled across nearly his entire upper back.

And this wolf was crowned.

Isla stared, unable to comprehend.

146

And then, in a blink, it was gone as he pulled on his shirt, buttoned it, knotted his cravat, shrugged on his coat. The floor creaked. The door opened, then shut with a soft click.

He had gone.

Isla was left behind the paravent.

Stunned. Shaken.

Barely believing what she had just seen.

Her knees gave way. She sank to the ground and pushed herself back until she felt the cold wall behind her.

She was shaking.

Her mind whirled like a fairground roundabout at Bartholomew Fair, spinning, refusing to settle, refusing to believe what she just saw.

Until, at last, a single thought surfaced. One that struck her with dawning horror.

The sweet man she'd promised to marry was, quite possibly, the most dangerous man in England.

Chapter Fourteen

TEDDY? *Her* Teddy? Gentle, earnest, warm-eyed Teddy? The one who blushed when their hands brushed? The one whose singular, sole passion was horology and who was oblivious to anything else if it didn't involve clocks? The one who read every single wish from her eyes, was charmingly inept when it came to dancing, fed her ices, chocolates and marzipan confections, and chased down half the country to find rare flowers simply because she'd once mentioned she liked them?

He had kissed her so passionately in Vauxhall Gardens.

A hot shiver ran through her as she remembered his ardour.

He'd declared he loved her. Deeply. Sincerely, like no man had ever done before. There'd been nothing but honesty in his eyes.

Isla was sitting at her toilette table, staring into the mirror without seeing anything.

Was that all a lie?

"M'lady. M'lady!" Meggie's voice emerged through the thick fog of her tumultuous thoughts. "Why don't ye let me brush yer hair?"

Isla blinked. For how long had she been sitting with her hand half-way lifted to her head, holding the brush?

Meggie pried the brush from her clutching fingers and brushed her hair with vigorous strokes.

Isla's thoughts went back to the room, to what she'd witnessed. After Teddy had left, she had remained sitting on the ground for a good ten minutes more, incapable of doing anything at all.

Until Meggie had finally slipped into the room to enquire what was the matter.

"Did you see Lord Linwood leave the room just now?"

"Linwood?" Meggie stared. "No. Why'd 'e be in there?"

Isla closed her eyes. Maybe he hadn't been. Maybe her mind had played tricks on her. Maybe she'd imagined it all.

"I've changed my mind. I won't be going out tonight after all," she'd managed to say in measured tones.

Meggie nodded, satisfied. "'Tis better that way, m'lady. The weather's awfully dreich tonight."

Isla had returned to her room.

But the whirl in Isla's brain refused to calm down.

A snarling wolf with a crown.

Lucian Night.

No, no, it was all a mistake. It couldn't possibly be true. Her imagination was running wild. It simply couldn't be. There must be another explanation. Anyone could have a tattoo. And anyone could have a wolf tattoo. Why not? It didn't have to mean anything. After all, the man she'd stabbed also had one. Who knew, maybe it was a popular motif, currently in fashion. Very likely, every second mariner had one. Why not Teddy, too?

It didn't have to mean anything.

But what if it did?

Back in St Giles, hadn't they all receded from him, avoiding him, fawning when a confrontation was inevitable? She'd thought nothing of it. She'd believed that was how commoners behaved when confronted with the aristocracy. But what if she was wrong? What if it was because they'd recognised him? What if it was because they feared him?

The boy. The innkeeper. The people who withdrew as soon as they'd approached as if they were the plague personified—it hadn't been normal behaviour, not in St Giles. Had they been told to stay out of their path?

Aside from the boy, not a single person had accosted them, and the streets had been empty as if a pestilence had wiped the entire quarter out.

Because they'd been in his territory. And they acknowledged him as their king.

The Lord of the Underworld.

Her heart was pounding violently, and she felt dizzy.

"Are ye all right?" Meggie asked for the third time after she finished binding her hair up in a simple chignon.

"No." Isla rubbed her forehead.

"Should I let his lordship know that yer not comin' fer dinner?"

Isla shook her head. She had to talk to Algie. Now.

Sofi Laporte

She got up and chose a dress, any dress. It didn't matter. She pulled out something from her clothes press without looking at what it was.

"Ye can't wear that. It's a riding habit." Meggie took it from her hands and pulled out a dark blue silk dress instead.

Meggie helped her get dressed, cursing all the while, lifting Isla's arms like a doll's as she pulled the dress over her head, since Isla was standing stiffly and uncooperatively, staring into space.

"There." Meggie tugged at the skirt and adjusted the neckline. "That's better."

"Thank you, Meggie," Isla said monotonously, and proceeded to the door.

"Your shoes!" Meggie held out a pair of silken slippers. "Or do ye want to go barefoot?"

"That's right," Isla said. "Shoes."

Meggie shook her head. "Maybe it's better to stay here if yer in such a state." She placed her hand on Isla's forehead. "Though ye don't seem to have no fever. There's the flux goin' about, so better stay in bed if yer feelin' ill."

"I'm all right, Meggie. Thank you."

Algie. She had to talk to Algie at once.

"Ah, Pixiekins," Algie said, taking off his monocle when she entered the room. "Just in time for supper."

"Indeed," Isla said as she folded her hands in front of her, not giving away with as much as a blink of an eyelash that her entire world had tilted on its axis only moments earlier.

"I just wanted to tell you I have no appetite at all, and I wanted to excuse myself from supper. But I would like to talk to you."

Algie lifted an eyebrow. "You are unwell? How can that be? You normally have the constitution of a seasoned warhorse. Nothing and nobody can bring you down. When the entire household had the influenza last winter, you were annoyingly chipper, the only one unaffected."

Isla gave him a weak smile.

"Besides," Algie continued, "we shall have a guest tonight for supper." He gestured at the armchair in the room's corner, a little in the shadow, from which someone rose.

Isla's stomach made a sickened lurch.

"Teddy," she whispered.

He beamed at her.

Isla swallowed.

"As you can see, I've invited Linwood tonight."

"We had some matters to discuss regarding our wedding," Teddy put in. "You won't believe how much paperwork one must wade through before one may get married in this country." He shook his head.

"One might as well save some time and have that conversation over supper." Algie indicated at the door to the dining room, which the footman opened.

"Quite so," she said woodenly. She felt completely caught off-guard as she hadn't expected to see him. Not so soon, not so quickly. Not before she'd had the chance to sort through her mind and to understand exactly what she had seen.

Of course he was here. Where else would he be? He now wore formal evening clothes and looked like Teddy was supposed to look: polished, normal, his nice, inconspicuous, usual self. Not a hint of what lay underneath those few threads of fabric.

His dark hair was slicked back, and his spectacles glinted on his nose, which he pushed back with one finger. The dimples in his cheeks appeared as he smiled, shyly, as though he was truly pleased to see her.

Dear sweet heavens.

He would be there all evening. Sitting right across from her. Looking at her. Speaking to her.

It was imperative that he didn't discover anything was amiss.

Isla attempted to control her panic beneath a mask of calm.

She nodded and smiled. "How lovely," she heard herself say. "That will be delightful." She held out her hand to him and he took it, warm and secure, and squeezed it.

A lump formed in her throat. She swallowed and increased her smile. "Of course, if Teddy is here, then I must join you for supper."

Teddy looked at her with concern. "But truly, you are not falling ill? You look awfully pale. The night air at Vauxhall was rather fresh, after all. I worried you'd catch a cold."

"Isla never catches colds," Algie grumbled. "Not even

when she slept the entire night outside in the garden, when she was but a girl, pretending to live the gypsy life."

Teddy turned to look at her. "Truly?"

Isla played with her pearl necklace Meggie had had the foresight to sling around her neck. "It stayed with me from my time with the Rom. I sleep better outside in the fresh air. I also find it more comfortable to sleep on the hard ground than in a suffocating bed." Then she blushed as she realized what she'd just said. For heaven's sake, she must get a grip on herself and stop jabbering nonsense.

Teddy's eyes widened as he took in that piece of information, just as Algie let out a chortle. "Best not buy a wedding bed, old chap, if the plain floor will do just as well." He clapped Teddy on the shoulder with such unexpected force that he stumbled forward.

"Algie. Really." Isla had gone bright scarlet, and so had Teddy. Now neither of them dared to meet the other's eye. For a blessed second only, she felt Teddy was still her Teddy, that nothing at all had changed between them, and all was good with the world.

The butler entered to announce that dinner was served, and she hesitated.

"Isla?" Both men were looking at her.

There was nothing in the world that she wanted to do more than to run away and hide, to crawl into her big bed and pull the blanket over her head and pretend it had never happened. She could stay in denial, to pretend she'd seen none of it. She'd hallucinated and imagined it all.

But if she withdrew now, if she excused herself and

returned to her room, that would be cowardly. She would be running from him and hiding.

And she would miss out on an excellent opportunity to discover what on earth was happening, and how it could be that from one moment to the next, her entire world had tilted, and she hadn't found her bearing yet.

What was happening?

Why?

Who was Teddy, really?

Surely, her brother must know?

What she needed the most, now, was answers. And not to run away and hide.

She pulled herself up. "I beg your pardon. I have been gathering wool. Let us have supper. I am famished."

SHE SAT down with them at the lavishly set supper table.

For when Algie supped, it was always lavish. All the silverware and crystal were out, the wine glasses were filled, the footmen served an elaborate six-course meal.

The men talked, and Isla strove to hide her shaking hand as she spooned the White Soup the footman had placed in front of her, normally her favourite, but now she barely tasted it.

She watched Teddy unabashedly as he conversed with Algie; always correct and polite with a dash of bashfulness, the dimple in his cheek appearing and disappearing as he talked, smiled, chewed and swallowed.

She furrowed her brows and took a sip from her water glass, turning her gaze away so she could concentrate on his voice.

It was different—so different.

Lucian Night's voice had been sharp. Cold. Sarcastic.

Teddy's was hesitant. Gentle. Almost shy.

They couldn't be more different from night and day, fire and ice, satin and steel.

But the *quality* of the voice, the pitch, was the same.

They shared the same tenor.

But was it the same voice, really? Her gaze returned once more to his face.

Teddy, sensing that she was watching him, looked up, and their eyes met. A smile tugged at the corner of his mouth, and he gave her a quick wink.

It was such a Teddy-like thing to do, playful and unexpected; and it was difficult not to smile back. She tore her eyes away and when she was served a plate full of fowl, she cut it into tiny and tinier pieces with concentration, quite forgetting to put anything into her mouth.

She must have been mistaken. Just because Teddy had a tattoo didn't mean that he was a criminal master-mind. It was absurd; entirely impossible.

Besides, there wasn't any other proof.

But what if he was a consummate actor? What if he was disguising himself as much as she'd been disguising herself as a boy?

What had that outfit been? A costermonger?

"What do you think, Pixiekins?" Algie turned to her.

I think that Teddy is Lucian Night, she nearly blurted out, but thankfully, she bit on her tongue. She picked up her glass and took a big sip, swallowed, coughed, and bought herself more time.

"You mean about Linwood's home?" She'd picked up that much of their conversation, thankfully.

"I was inquiring how you feel about establishing yourself at Linwood's estate. It's surrounded by moors and mist, which strikes me as rather melancholy." Algie shook his head with disapproval.

"Most certainly, it is not," Teddy interjected, jabbing his fork into the air for emphasis. "The manor house sits high upon a hill overlooking the sea, and one feels a sense of liberation when gazing upon the waters."

"Liberation," Isla echoed.

"Yes. I care little for confining, constricting spaces."

Like the constricting cells of Newgate prison.

Or the feeling of the noose as it tightened about one's neck.

Isla rubbed her neck and shifted in her seat.

"The cliffs are magnificent," Teddy continued. "The villages are charming, and the sea is the most exquisite shade of azure imaginable."

When he spoke like that, with the eagerness and easy ingenuity of someone entirely without secrets, he seemed much younger than he was.

Definitely not a criminal mastermind.

"And not a soul to be seen for miles on those dreary, endless Yorkshire moors," Algie added, holding out his wineglass to be refilled.

"True," Teddy said with a nod. "The moors are quite something. A man might easily lose his way on them. They keep their secrets well."

Isla's gaze flew to him. "Secrets? What secrets?"

Teddy gave a little shrug. "Oh, anything, really. Things tend to disappear out there. The moors are notorious for hiding...all sorts of things."

Isla choked.

Perhaps he was a criminal mastermind after all.

"Smugglers," Algie mused. "They liked to hide on the moors. Until we sniffed them out, that is. Don't worry, Isla, it is quite safe now. I personally shall make sure that it is."

Somehow, that didn't comfort Isla in the least.

Teddy turned to Isla with a laugh. "I promise you, there are no smugglers or pirates or other unsavoury characters anywhere near Roseview Mansion. It is as safe there as your brother's house here."

"How comforting to know." She gave him a tremulous smile.

"It shall be my pleasure to show you my home, which shall soon be yours, too."

"Has the property been in your family for long?" Isla enquired politely.

"Not at all. I acquired it recently. I saw the property on my last trip up to Scotland, and it was for sale."

"And you just bought it." Algie commented. "Because you wanted it."

"Naturally."

"Commendable."

Teddy shrugged. "When I want something, I usually get it. And once it is mine, it stays mine forever." His eyes locked with Algie's.

And then she saw it.

A sliver of ice.

A calculating, steely resolve that lay behind the sleepy, good-natured mask he wore.

Isla shuddered as if the winds of the North Pole had swept through their dining room.

Teddy turned to her, his eyes having returned to their familiar, guileless expression.

"You certainly seem to be a man who knows what he wants," Algie stated sleepily, as if he'd not noticed anything unusual at all.

Isla put down her glass carefully, and shook her head when the footman offered to refill it. "It sounds most agreeable, indeed, and I shall look forward to beholding your, that is, our home," she said in a formal tone.

Teddy, however, did not notice anything amiss and kept talking about his estate, describing in great detail the natural habitat, not caring that neither of his parties were listening. Algie was too busy focusing on eating his fowl, whereas Isla was staring at his animated face but not taking in any of his words. She watched his lips move.

Those lips that had kissed with such passion.

"I want your first kiss."

The words echoed in her memory as clearly and sharply as if Teddy had said them aloud in the dining room.

She dropped the spoon to the ground with a loud clank. Isla bent to pick it up before the footman could intervene. When she lifted her upper body and her head, she felt oddly light.

"Are you well, Isla?" Algie demanded for the fourth time that evening.

"I do think it would be best for me to retire," Isla finally admitted. She'd reached the end of her tether. She needed distance and quiet to think it through. She needed to escape the watchful eyes of Algie, and the solicitous, warm ones of Teddy.

She needed time to think.

BACK IN HER ROOM, after Meggie had helped her into her nightgown and brushed her red hair to a coppery shine, Isla crawled into her bed.

Her mind was no longer reeling.

It had fixated itself on a single thought.

He'd demanded her first kiss. As part of their contract.

With an arrogant confidence, she'd brushed it off as meaningless.

Then she'd given her first kiss to Teddy.

And she'd been so glad that it had been him, and not —*him*. She'd gleefully believed she'd outwitted him, even.

She shot upright in bed.

"Oh, the nerve of the man!"

Finally, the confusion lifted, and an emotion shot through her, one she greeted with such relief that she almost sobbed: anger.

How *dare* he deceive her so?

How dare he play with her?

How dare he lie?

How dare he play cat and mouse with her?

She clenched her fingers. She was Lady Isla Rothvale, sister of Lord Algernon Wynthorpe.

Isla formed a resolution.

She would obtain proof of his identity, incontrovertible proof, and she would have him convicted. She would beat him at his own game.

And with that resolution firmly in her mind, she finally fell asleep.

Chapter Fifteen

THE NEXT MORNING AT BREAKFAST, Isla attempted to broach the subject of Teddy, hoping to discover how much Algie truly knew of him.

Yet it proved quite futile, rather like attempting to breach a fortress wall.

She knew that her brother was no fool. If Teddy really was Lucian Night, surely her brother would be aware of it? This, alone, prompted so many other questions that Isla began to feel her head throb.

He must have known, perhaps from the very beginning.

Then why, in heaven's name, did he allow Lucian Night into his home? Why did he conduct furtive conversations with the man in the dead of night within the library? Why had he not only allowed, but actively encouraged her betrothal to his adversary, the very man he had been pursuing with such determination? Why was he marrying his only sister to his enemy? Surely, he couldn't be earnest about this union. What did he hope to achieve through such an arrangement?

Why?

Isla tried to broach the subject the very next morning, while Algie was consuming a hefty slab of roast beef, his customary breakfast fare.

But every time she brought up the topic of Lucian Night, Algie would have none of it. He raised a hand. "I'd rather you no longer mention that accursed name in this house, particularly not during a meal. It gives me a migraine, nausea and indigestion."

"The thing is," Isla persisted, ignoring her brother's protests, "I was wondering what you would do if you were to finally apprehend him."

"I should see him hanged. Once and for all." He attacked his beef with such ferocity, as if it were Lucian Night himself. "And this time it would be permanent."

Isla looked at her brother in bewilderment. Then why didn't he? Doubt crept over her again. Could there be another explanation for Teddy's tattoo?

She tried a different approach. "Very well. You're right, it's an unsavoury topic for breakfast. Let us speak of something else. I am curious about your thoughts on body art. Made in ink. Tattoos."

Algie glanced up. "Such as the sailors have?"

"Yes. I have discovered that many more people have them. Often the very people one would never expect." She hesitated. "Do you recall the man I thought I had killed?" She took a big breath. "He had one too. Upon his wrist, of a wolf."

Algie never stopped eating. "Did he, now? I suppose

that explains your obsession with Lucian Night. You wish to know whether the man who bore that mark could have been him."

Isla looked at him expectantly. "Yes. That is it."

"How exceedingly clever of you it would have been, had that been the case," her brother mused. "You would have rendered me a considerable service, to be sure. But, alas, Pixiekins, that tattoo happens to be common. Ever since Lucian Night became notorious and adopted it as his personal mark, people have been emulating him and inking the deuced wolf all over themselves." He continued with his meal.

The small spoon she'd been holding fell out of her hand. "You mean to say that just because someone has that tattoo, it doesn't mean they're a criminal?"

Algie laughed. "I wish it were so! Imagine us locking up everyone who bears the tattoo of the wolf. But the truth is that it's quite fashionable these days. Shall I confess something that I learned just recently?" He leaned forward with a grin. "Lord Mountbatten has one, too."

"What? A tattoo of a wolf?" Isla asked, breathless.

"Indeed." Algie chuckled into his wine. "Would you believe it? Starchy and proper on the surface like a Methodist preacher, but as soon as he takes off his coat, he's inked like a common sailor from the Indies. Confessed it to me himself the other day, when he was well into his cups."

"Oh!" Isla sank back into her chair. "So, it is entirely fashionable these days—" her voice shook "—and there is nothing to it at all when gentlemen mark their bodies with these kinds of symbols."

"Nothing at all, my dear sister, nothing at all." Algie was still chuckling and shaking his head.

"I see."

The relief that swept through her left her light-headed. Tears sprang into her eyes, and she dabbed with her napkin at them, smiling.

"Of course. How excessively foolish of me." She drew in a steadying breath. "I am so glad."

"About what?" Algie lifted a finger, and the footman removed the plate and served the pudding.

Isla suddenly noticed that her appetite had returned, and she dug into the lemon custard with renewed enthusiasm.

"Nothing of consequence. I am simply glad."

"Ah yes, thus speaks the happy bride."

"Yes." Her forehead puckered together. "But, Algie, don't you agree that Linwood's behaviour has been somewhat peculiar lately?"

He paused, his loaded spoon halfway to his mouth. "In what manner?"

She opened her mouth.

In what manner, indeed? Truth be told, there was nothing in his behaviour that was suspicious, merely the fact that he wore a tattoo. Which, as Algie had just stated, seemed to be the very rage these days.

And that she had seen him in a state of undress.

Isla shifted uncomfortably in her chair.

"Because he, too, has a—a—"

"He has bats in his belfry?" Algie snorted.

Isla folded her arms across her chest and studied her brother. "Pray, Algie. Why did you consent to my marrying him if you don't like him?"

"Never said I don't like him," he mumbled.

"No, but you make it clear every time I bring him up. And yesterday at supper, you were not the politest to him, either."

"I am impatient with people who have maggots in their heads. In this case," he said in-between two sips of port, "it is clocks rather than maggots."

"But—"

"But!" He lifted a finger. "He's a good sort of fellow, otherwise, even if one has the impression that his upper storey is yawningly empty." He tapped a finger against his temple. "But you're to marry him. We have agreed to advance the wedding to a fortnight's time." He nodded as if the matter were final.

"What?" Isla lowered her spoon. "A fortnight? So soon?"

Algie pulled out his pocket watch. "Yes. Appears to be in a dashed hurry to wed you, which may not be entirely disadvantageous. Now speaking of being in a hurry, if you don't mind, I really must go." Algie pushed back his chair. "Dashed pressed for time."

Algie left, leaving Isla alone.

"Would you care to take tea in the drawing room, my lady?" Falks, the butler, asked.

"No, thank you." She felt emotionally drained now that the tension she'd carried with her ever since she'd seen Teddy without his shirt had dissolved in such an unremarkable fashion.

"Lord Linwood has sent word that he will come to call this afternoon."

"Thank you, Falks." She returned to her room to rest, her heart thumping erratically at the prospect of seeing Teddy again so soon.

How foolish of her to have leapt to such conclusions, she berated herself.

Poor Teddy. He didn't deserve her unfounded suspicions.

Chapter Sixteen

"I HAD HOPED to escort you to Madame Tussaud's exhibition of waxworks," Teddy informed her upon his arrival that afternoon. "But alas, she is currently touring the provinces. So instead, I have another destination in mind."

In place of wax figures, he brought her to *Professor Maker's Marvellous Mechanical Menagerie*—an itinerant exhibition housed in a striped pavilion near the bustling market stalls of Covent Garden. Inside were automata, scientific curiosities, and clever optical illusions. Catherine accompanied them as chaperone.

The show was, to Isla's surprise, thoroughly delightful.

There were clockwork toys and lifelike mechanical figures that performed tunes on tiny instruments, alongside more scholarly contraptions: telescopes, pneumatic pumps, and a 'magic lantern' that cast eerie images onto a canvas screen.

Teddy's particular favourite, however, was the orrery: a splendid brass model used to calculate the movements of planets and moons.

He launched into a detailed explanation of its workings, eyes bright with enthusiasm. Isla listened with a smile on her face, though the intricacies of gears and rotations quite escaped her understanding. She'd watched Teddy the entire time, and doubtless he must have noticed, for he smiled back every time their eyes met. Once he lifted her hand and pressed a quick kiss on it, which caused her to blush. She was wearing gloves, so there was no reason at all for her heart to thump the way it did, she chided herself.

"'Tis a pity your brother is not here to see this. He would have found it most entertaining," Catherine remarked when they finally left the exhibition.

Isla threw her a surprised look. "Yes, I suppose he would have. Particularly the mechanical toys. Algie can be ridiculously childish sometimes."

"Though I suppose a man like him would never have time for entertainment like this. He is a thoroughly busy man." Catherine's face appeared serene, though Isla detected a faint note of wistfulness lacing her voice.

Isla halted and looked her fully in the face. "Catherine. Never say you like my brother?"

Catherine started visibly. "What a peculiar question! Whatever would prompt you to ask such a thing?" Without awaiting Isla's response, she rushed on. "Of course I like him. He is a very likeable man. He must be liked by many people." A delicate flush crept up her cheeks.

Isla took her arm and grinned. "Ooh. Yes, of course. He is very well liked. Exceptionally so. It is therefore entirely meaningless if you, too, like him."

"What complete nonsense you talk sometimes, Isla." Catherine fanned herself with one hand. "Look there! I behold Lady Wentgrove. I must speak to her. Pray excuse me for a moment? I shall return presently." Catherine fled.

"It appears you have touched a sore point," Teddy murmured close to her ear.

Isla started, for she hadn't noticed him approach. He offered his arm. "Shall we investigate the antiquities shop over there, whilst we wait? It appears they sell some interesting clocks." He lifted his stick to point at a little corner shop in a narrow lane.

Isla nodded.

The shop was bigger than the exterior suggested, and seemed to be connected with the adjacent buildings, consisting of a series of rooms, each dedicated to different categories of objects. One room contained old books. The second room furniture, such as sedans, chairs and escritoires; the third clocks of all shapes and sizes; and the fourth, the most distant and shadowy, held an assortment of curiosities that Isla found fascinating. While Teddy immersed himself in investigating the timepieces in the third room, Isla studied the bric-a-brac that was collected in the last room.

She discovered a little musical box and lifted the lid. A tiny bird emerged, and a tinkling melody played. It was charming. The entire shelf was filled with similar musical boxes. Isla wondered whether she should buy one when she noticed that next to the shelf was a curtain concealing what appeared to be a doorway. And since the curtain fluttered, the passage seemed to be open.

Curious whether it led to yet another room with oddities, Isla drew the curtain aside and entered.

She found herself in a dim, sparsely furnished room, with only a rickety table and several chairs. What appeared to be a map lay spread upon the table, and the men seated around it looked up in surprise.

She had clearly intruded upon private quarters. Isla froze in mortification. "Oh. I do beg your pardon. I believed this to be another room belonging to the antiquities shop."

She turned to go, but one of the men lurched forward, blocking her path. "Not so hasty." He grinned, revealing a set of blackened teeth. Isla recoiled.

"Ye can't just waltz in 'ere like that."

"As I explained, it was a mistake. Now, if you would permit me to—" Isla backed away, and the man made a motion as if to grab her. Alarmed, Isla spun about and crashed into a rock.

A band of steel wrapped around her. "Careful."

Teddy.

"What's this?" He looked around with curiosity.

The man who had approached her stopped, then slammed the door shut. In the semi- dark, Isla perceived that he held a weapon. Her own fingers tightened around her umbrella.

"Well, well, well, who have we here?" drawled a tall, bald man who looked like a mariner. "A tulip." He smirked.

Teddy blinked. Then he cocked a smile. "'Tis actually a camellia." He indicated the flower adorning his buttonhole, which was currently all the rage. "Though I wouldn't expect simple mariners like you to know that."

Isla regarded him with astonishment. It wasn't like Teddy to be so aggressive.

"I think we should leave," Isla whispered to him. But Teddy didn't appear to hear.

To her amazement, he strolled further into the room. "It's a most interesting place, don't you agree? Furniture, clocks, and now—maps?" He tilted his head thoughtfully. "I happen to like old maps. May I have a look? Ah, the Thames."

One of the men hastily rolled up the map.

Teddy looked at them with a smirk. "Surely you are not affiliated with those river pirates one hears such tales about. What are they called again?" He snapped a finger. "Something with skulls."

They jumped up with a snarl.

"Teddy," Isla repeated, not daring to move, for the ruffian, who held a long, ugly blade in his hand, crept closer, and two of the other vile looking men had also pulled weapons out of their shirts. They were surrounded.

And Teddy, apparently oblivious, wouldn't stop provoking them without the slightest sign of alarm.

"Take 'im," one commanded.

The three men lunged at Teddy, who ducked. Then pandemonium erupted.

Isla had no idea what happened, but she had no intention of being murdered. She rammed the end of the umbrella into the assailant's midsection so that he doubled over. Then she rushed to the door, flung it wide, and hollered in her loudest voice, "Help!"

The entire altercation didn't last longer than a few seconds.

When she turned again to check on Teddy, the scene had changed entirely.

All four men lay in a heap on the floor. Only one of them groaned. That was the fellow she'd poked with the umbrella. The remaining three were ominously still.

Teddy stood in their midst, gazing down at them, gripping his walking stick.

Isla stared in amazement.

He looked up apologetically and gestured with his stick. "You took care of one fellow. Two managed to knock their heads together, and the third—" he made a helpless motion with his stick "—somehow fell over."

"Fell over," Isla echoed faintly.

"So it would appear." Teddy looked down at the fallen men pensively. He prodded one of the bodies with his boot. "You don't suppose they're dead?"

"Merciful heavens. Are they, really? What are we to do now?"

Rapid footsteps approached.

The proprietor of the antiquities shop burst into the room. "I heard noises. Customers are not permitted in this room. Didn't you see the sign outsi—" He broke off when he beheld the scene, then shut the door firmly. "What in blazes happened?"

Teddy retrieved the map that had rolled under the table and brushed it off. "There was a bit of a scuffle."

The shopkeeper scowled. "I can see that. Who are you?" His hand moved toward his waistcoat as though reaching for a pistol.

"Linwood is my name." Teddy lifted both his hands in appeasement. "And this is Lady—"

"It was self-defence," Isla interrupted. "I believed this room to be part of your establishment. These men, for no reason at all, became most threatening and drew weapons. And, and—" she made a helpless motion "—then somehow this occurred," she ended lamely.

But the shopkeeper wasn't listening. He continued staring at Teddy.

Or more precisely, on the head of his walking stick, just visible where Teddy's hand gripped the shaft. It gleamed in the dim light.

The man paled visibly. He moistened his lips. "There appears to have been a misunderstanding."

"A misunderstanding. That's a way of putting it." Teddy nodded gravely.

"But—" Isla began.

"I offer my most profound apologies. This should never have happened."

"No, it should not have," Teddy agreed.

The shopkeeper escorted them from the room, bowing as he held the door open, apologising continuously as they traversed the shop, then holding the front door open for them.

"And those men?" Isla turned to the shopkeeper. "What will happen to them?"

"I'll take care of them. There is no cause whatsoever for concern."

"But—"

"Excellent," Teddy declared and took Isla's arm with a firm grip and steered her to their carriage.

"You are unharmed?" He framed her face gently, turning it from this way to that, checking for any injuries.

"Yes. But, Teddy—"

He examined her hand, her arm, then the other.

"I'm perfectly well," Isla assured him with a small laugh. "Truly, I am."

He released her.

"You overcame those ruffians single-handedly," Isla said. "It is true you have been training with Gentleman Jackson."

He flexed his fingers and shot her a quick grin. "Indeed, I have. That's a formidable weapon you have there." He pointed at her umbrella, which now rested next to his walking stick. He'd set it aside immediately after they'd entered the carriage.

Isla picked up his stick and turned it in her hands.

"As is this?"

"Those men were the most discourteous customers. Really. The shopkeeper must do something about it."

"Teddy..." Isla stared at the silver head adorning his stick, her heart racing. Teddy was watching her, a faint smile curving his lips.

"Who can say how many customers they have driven away?"

"Tell me, Teddy." She was surprised that her voice remained steady. "Are you fond of wolves?"

She raised the stick, showing the gleaming visage of the snarling wolf at the handle.

"Not particularly," Teddy replied with easy composure, settling back in his seat. "You refer to the wolf's head?"

She nodded.

"'Tis merely decorative. There was a choice between a lion, an elephant, and a wolf. In silver or gold. I selected the silver wolf."

"For no reason other than that you liked it."

"Precisely."

Surely many walking sticks bore wolf-shaped handles. It did not have to mean anything. Algie had said as much that such things were quite fashionable these days. Any gentleman might possess such a stick.

And Teddy had admitted he boxed with Gentleman Jackson himself, no less. That would explain how he had dispatched those ruffians in the shop with such speed and precision.

Boxing, too, was much in vogue among gentlemen. Perfectly unremarkable.

Isla found herself on the verge of asking whether that was also the reason he bore a wolf's head tattooed between his shoulder blades, but that would land her in a rather awkward position, since it would require admitting she had seen him in a state of undress.

She remembered the warmth of his skin, the way his muscles had shifted as he moved. A wave of heat rose to her cheeks.

Isla set the stick aside. "I see."

She clasped her hands to keep them still. They had grown quite cold.

"Shall we stop for some refreshments at Gunter's? I

vow I could benefit from a strong dose of sugar after all this excitement."

Isla shook her head. "I am feeling rather fatigued. Let us return home."

Teddy handed her down in front of her residence, concern on his brow. "I hope you're not falling ill. Last evening, as well, you mentioned feeling out of sorts."

"All I need is a little rest." She attempted a smile, but it came out rather wanly.

She turned to go, but he caught her hand, halting her.

"Open your umbrella," he said quietly.

"Why? It isn't raining..." The sudden intensity in his eyes made her pause. She obeyed.

In the next moment, he drew her against him, so swiftly the air rushed from her lungs, and then his lips found hers—urgent, unrelenting—as the umbrella shielded them from curious eyes.

They might have kissed for an eternity. The world had fallen away. No sound, no time, no place—only Teddy, and the joy of it, the sheer rightness of it, as if everything had been leading to this moment.

His mouth moved to her ear. "I wish... I wish..."

"What?" Her voice was breathless, rough with emotion.

"So very much..."

He drew her into a fierce embrace, her head pressed against his chest, where his heartbeat as wildly as her own. One hand stroked her hair, slow and steady.

She had never felt so completely held. So safe. As though nothing could reach her; not fear, not doubt, not the past.

He felt like home.

He lifted his hand to her cheek, his touch unbearably tender. His eyes searched hers, full of unspoken questions.

"I wish you would trust me more," he whispered.

The words were so soft, she almost thought she'd imagined them.

She parted her lips. "I do."

The truth of it struck her the moment the words left her mouth.

It sounded like a vow.

It felt like a vow.

Teddy felt it too. His eyes lit with a fierce, unguarded joy that stole her breath.

He opened his mouth to reply—

But the front door creaked open, and Falks, the butler, appeared on the threshold. "My lord. My lady." He cleared his throat delicately. "If you require more time—"

Teddy and Isla looked at each other, eyes brimming with suppressed laughter.

"He has undoubtedly been watching us through the window this entire time," Teddy observed. "The rascal." He let her go, though with evident reluctance.

Isla coloured, a bloom of happiness and embarrassment warming her cheeks. "Will you be joining us for supper this evening?"

"Naturally." His gaze softened. "This evening and every evening."

She climbed the steps to her door, where Falks waited with his usual patient dignity. But just before she crossed the threshold, Isla glanced over her shoulder.

There was Teddy, alone on the pavement, executing a small, joyful jig.

A laugh bubbled up and escaped her, light and bright as springtime.

MEGGIE WAS CHATTING about this and that, but Isla didn't hear a word of it.

After she disappeared, and Isla was clad in her night-gown, she draped a warm, woollen shawl over her shoulders and curled up in the armchair.

She felt as though she were floating on a cloud.

Teddy had come to supper, indeed, and sat next to her, and they'd held hands the entire time, while trying to eat their way through several courses. This presented certain challenges, as cutting the meat on her plate with only one hand proved difficult. Yet under no circumstances would she release Teddy's hand.

He had caressed the back of her hand with his thumb, sending delightful sparks through her entire being, and she'd barely been able to focus on the conversation.

Every time their gazes met, Teddy winked surreptitiously, causing bubbles of laughter to rise within her, and it was difficult to suppress while at the same time eating.

Finally, when the pudding was served, Algie released a big sigh and shook his head. "There is nothing more tiresome than dining with two besotted lovebirds," he declared with disgust. "Watching you two fairly destroys my appetite." He pushed his plate away.

"Why?" Isla looked at him with innocent eyes. "We have merely been eating as usual, Teddy and I. Have we not?"

Teddy's eyes were equally innocent. "Indeed. It has been a most delicious meal of, er, lamb."

"Veal," Algie growled. "We ate veal." He pointed a finger at him. "You're so besotted with my sister that you don't even know what you're putting into your mouth."

Their eyes met once more, and the look of guilt on Teddy's face was so endearing that Isla's shoulders shook with suppressed mirth.

They had been unable to converse properly afterwards, occupied as they were with gazing into each other's eyes and giggling.

Algie threw up his hands in exasperation and withdrew, and Teddy, too, departed after an extended farewell. Reaching the front door had never required so much time, with stolen kisses, eye gazing and even more kisses.

Isla had fairly floated up the stairs afterward.

The smile she'd given Teddy when he finally left was still on her face.

So this was what love felt like?

She'd always assumed it would be fireworks and excitement and sizzling. And while she'd experienced that, too, this feeling, with Teddy, was more grounded, as though he anchored her, as though he truly perceived her essence, which was nothing like she'd ever experienced before. It was calmer, more stable, safer.

It felt like coming home.

And they would wed.

Isla counted the days.

In less than a fortnight.

She sighed contentedly.

In less than a fortnight, they would belong to each other forever.

Chapter Seventeen

THE FOLLOWING days were a flurry of activity. There was so much to accomplish before the wedding! The trousseau required preparation. China, silver, fabric, clothes, jewellery—the list was endless. Teddy called daily, with a thousand questions regarding the redecoration of their home. He did not want to undertake anything without consulting her first; he declared. From the colour of the wallpaper in their future drawing room to the type of wood she preferred for her clothing press, the decisions that had to be made were quite endless.

One afternoon, he arrived with three massive clocks, which he set up on the drawing room table.

"I could not decide, so I purchased all three," he explained. "But now comes the dilemma: where to put them?"

Isla examined the clocks, two of which were mantelpiece pieces, and the third designed to hang on a wall. She reached out to touch one clock and brushed his hand, and Teddy immediately took advantage, drawing her into his arms. One thing led to another, and it was only when Falks cleared his throat loudly behind them, a good while later, that they jumped apart.

"As—as I was saying," Teddy said sheepishly, "the clocks."

"Yes." They both glanced at Falks, who walked up to the cabinet to take out the silver.

"One in each drawing room," Isla decided.

Teddy inclined his head. "We possess only one, not three, like you're used to in Algie's spacious townhouse. But we can put them all in there, if you wish."

"That would be perfectly agreeable."

They looked at each other happily.

LATER THAT AFTERNOON, Isla had an appointment with Catherine to visit the Foundling Hospital at Coram's Fields, one of the charitable endeavours that was dear to Isla's heart. She had hoped that Teddy might accompany them, but to her disappointment, he was unable to join them.

"I have a prior engagement," he said with a rueful expression. "I shall miss you dreadfully, and I shall count every minute until we may be together again."

Catherine arrived, and they departed at the same time. Isla waited until Teddy took his leave and waved farewell to him.

"You appear to be deeply in love," Catherine observed later, in their carriage, as they travelled to the Foundling Hospital. "I confess I am envious."

Isla placed both hands against her cheeks. "Is it so very obvious?"

"Indeed. More than obvious. You have stars in your eyes. How fortunate you are to marry someone you love." Catherine toyed with the fringes of her reticule. "The rest of us are not that lucky."

Her own marriage to her late husband had been a union arranged by her parents.

Isla took Catherine's hand in hers and squeezed it gently. "I wish, more than anything in this world, that you, my dearest friend, might experience this happiness as well."

Catherine returned the pressure. "Thank you," she whispered.

The visit occupied the entire afternoon, so by the time they departed, dusk had fallen. Their carriage waited before the iron gates of the building when a second carriage arrived, and the Dowager Countess Redgrave alighted—Catherine's mother-in-law.

"So one must come all the way to the orphanage in order to get a glimpse of you," Lady Redgrave said. She was a cold, proud woman and Isla did not like her at all. That was one trial she was to be spared: a mother-in-law. Though she would dearly have loved having a mother, being unable to recall her own, and missing Lady Wynthorpe, who had been as a mother to her all these years.

It was evident that Lady Redgrave's and Catherine's relationship was strained.

Catherine turned to Isla with a pained expression. "I am sorry, Isla. But I think I need to go with my mother-in-law. We have matters to discuss. Please take my carriage home. I'll instruct John to take you there directly."

Isla waved her concern away. "Do not trouble yourself about me in the least. I shall go straight home and retire, for I am both tired and quite famished."

Catherine pressed her hands, then climbed into Lady Redgrave's carriage, while Isla climbed into Catherine's vehicle, glad to be on her way home.

The carriage rumbled along, and Isla settled back with a smile on her face, thinking of Teddy. She composed mental lists of tasks that still had to be done, articles to be purchased, and furniture to be arranged. Her heart quickened at the thought that the day was coming soon.

Five days. She counted them on her fingers.

In five days, they would be wed.

Could there be any greater happiness?

She dozed and awoke as the carriage came to an abrupt halt.

"Begging your pardon, my lady." John had descended and opened the door. "But there has been an accident ahead. And with Tottenham Court Road blocked as well, we must take a different route. It'll take longer to reach Mayfair."

"That is quite all right, John. There is no hurry," Isla replied.

Night had fallen, and their progress was exceedingly slow.

She gazed from the window and realised they were passing through St Giles. That was indeed a detour.

There stood the Angel Inn. With a smile on her face, she remembered how she'd dragged Teddy there. How long ago that seemed!

Isla sat forward and blinked.

She'd been thinking so intently about Teddy that he appeared to have materialised before her. For there he was, striding down a side alley, his cloak billowing behind him.

Teddy.

It was his figure, his bearing, his attire, his hat.

Perhaps not his usual gait, because Teddy was inclined to amble leisurely along as he twirled his walking stick, rather than stride purposefully down a dark, squalid alley...with everyone leaping out of his path or pressing themselves against the walls, or even halting to bow respectfully as if he were... The Lord of St Giles himself.

"I shall return presently," Isla called to John, opened the door, and went after Teddy.

ISLA WAS glad she'd worn sensible walking boots and a simple, dark cloak that day. She drew the hood over her head and slipped into the shadows, pretending to know exactly where she was going.

She gripped her umbrella for good measure, but she wasn't accosted by anyone, and people paid no heed to her as they, too, hurried past. The fog was beginning to rise, and she knew that shortly it would be impossible to see anything at all in the streets.

Hurrying after Teddy, she glimpsed his coat billow as he turned into an even narrower alley, then vanish through a doorway.

Isla paused in front of the door, which bore the crude image of the wolf painted in red. Her hand lifted to knock, then fell as she pushed gently at the door, which yielded.

She found herself in a dark, narrow courtyard belonging to some manner of a warehouse. All the windows were dark save for one row on the ground floor at the far side of the courtyard.

Pressing herself against the shadowed wall, Isla pulled her hood low over her brow and crept toward the grimy windows. She raised herself just enough to peer within.

The room beyond was stripped bare, its only furnishing a single armchair positioned directly in the centre. A row of rough-looking men stood behind it, arms folded, faces hard.

And in that chair, settling himself with a flourish and a flick of his coattails, Teddy sat.

A man knelt before him, bound hand and foot with coarse rope. Behind him loomed another group of ruffians, even more brutal in appearance than the first. The stench of the rookery clung to them—filth, smoke, and blood.

Isla edged closer, straining to listen.

Teddy spoke. "Seems we've got ourselves a traitor."

Merciful heavens, his voice! The same voice she'd heard in the gambling club. Colder than frostbite, and underneath the silky veneer, harsh and unrelenting and more cutting than steel.

Isla shuddered. She pressed a trembling fist to her mouth to stifle her gasp. Her heart pounded like thunder, and her knees buckled, but the wall supported her.

The bound man whimpered. "Ain't true, sir, swear it on me mum! It's all a bleedin' mistake! I didn't know they were Mudlark Skulls, I didn't! If I'd known, I'd never 'ave touched the job. Never!"

Teddy gave the slightest nod.

One of his men stepped forward and tossed a rolled sheet onto the floor beside the bound man. It landed with a thud.

Even in the dim light, Isla recognised it. The map. The same one she'd seen back at the antiquities shop with Teddy only days ago.

Teddy's voice dropped scarcely above a whisper, soft as smoke. "And what of this?"

The man recoiled. "Don't know nothin' about no map. Ain't mine, swear on me life. Never seen it before, I ain't." His voice cracked, almost a sob.

Teddy leaned in, elbow resting lazily on his knee. "Is that so? How curious. Because Tobbin and Leeks—" he gestured, and two men stepped forward, one squat and broad, the other tall and lean "—they swear they witnessed you make the deal. Swear it on their lives."

The bound man let out a wild shriek. "They're lyin'. Dirty bleedin' liars, the pair of 'em!"

"Are they?" Teddy barely stirred, but another man was dragged into view. His hands were bound tight behind his back.

Teddy turned to him. "Was it him?"

Silence.

A shove from behind made the man stumble. "Aye," he muttered at last. "It were him."

"It weren't," the first man cried. "He come to me, said I could earn a few coins on the side. I weren't tryin' to cross you, I swear on me sainted mum. I didn't mean no harm."

The room went still. No word from Teddy, no sign. But something must have passed between Teddy and his men, some silent form of communication.

Two of them stepped forward, seized the bound man under the arms, and dragged him away.

Isla panicked. She ducked behind a stack of crates, heart thundering.

The door creaked open. The men took him into the courtyard.

One of them drew a flintlock.

Cold horror dawned as Isla understood what would happen. She squeezed her eyes shut and pressed both hands over her ears.

But the shot still tore through the night like a thunderclap.

A considerable time passed.

When she finally dared to open her eyes, the courtyard was empty.

Her breath escaped in a strangled sob. She must compose herself. She must. She needed to leave this place, escape, find Algie.

Immediately.

Keeping low, she crept back along the wall the way she had come.

She found the main entrance, slipped through the door, and stumbled through the foggy alley, back to the road where John was waiting with the carriage.

Chapter Eighteen

ISLA WAS REELING with the impact of what she had just witnessed.

How could it be?

How was any of it possible?

Perhaps it was all a terrible dream. A nightmare. An illusion.

Everything—every smile, every sweet gesture, every word—had been a lie?

Her heart ached in ways she had never thought possible.

Yet...why was she so surprised? The signs had been there from the beginning. She had suspected that something was amiss with Teddy from the start. She had noticed real, tangible clues, and still she had looked away. She had chosen blissful ignorance, clinging to the belief that he truly was who he professed to be. Because she *wanted* him to be Teddy. Needed him to be Teddy. Thus, she ignored the truth, even as everything screamed in her face that he was not.

Until it was too late, and she had become a witness to a murder.

Isla paused before the door to Algie's study; her hand poised in the air. She lifted it once, then again, but allowed it to fall both times. Turning away, she climbed the staircase. She stopped halfway. After a moment of indecision, she turned and made her way back down again.

Why was she hesitating? She had always told Algie everything. There had never been any secrets between them. She had trusted Algie with her very soul, and she knew she was right to place such faith in him.

She took a breath, knocked briskly, and entered.

Algie sat at his desk, which was unusually free of oranges. He was examining a sheet of paper through a magnifying lens. When he looked up at her, he lowered the glass.

It was a map.

Her stomach lurched. She recognised it immediately. It was the very map from the antiquities shop, the one that had shown the territory of the Mudlark Skulls.

"Pixiekins," he said in a mild tone, "you ought to be in bed."

"I am quite well," she replied. "Or I shall be once we have spoken."

She crossed the room and sat opposite him, her hands clasped tightly in her lap.

Algie narrowed his gaze. "Something has happened. Tell me everything."

She did.

She told him everything from the moment she

accepted Teddy's proposal. How she had, at first, intended to use him to discover what had become of Jem. She described their visits to the rookery, the gambling hell, Lucian Night's disgraceful proposal, and the tattoo. She concealed nothing, save for the most terrible part. When it came to the moment in the warehouse, when he'd given the order to take a man's life, her voice faltered.

Algie listened in silence, his expression perfectly unreadable.

When she reached the end of her tale, he raised one brow, as though she had merely related a society column in *The Gazette*.

"Algie?" Her voice was uneven. Where was the fury, the indignation, the protective brother she had expected? There was only a small crease between his brows, the sole indication of deeper thought.

Then she understood.

She leaned back in the chair and exhaled. "You already knew everything."

Algie folded his hands atop the desk, saying nothing to confirm or deny her words. A slight flicker of regret crossed his features.

She pressed her fingers against her temples. "Of course you knew. You always know everything about everyone. Rather like Providence."

"Not quite. I know far less than that," he said, rising and strolling toward the fire. "And I would never presume to be Providence. Although, I do take some pride in my work."

For a moment, his lips curved in a small, satisfied smile before he concealed it.

"Algie."

He turned to face her, a worried fold between his brows. "I did not realise you had formed an attachment to Night. That was not our intention. We believed you would remain unaffected by him. That was part of the reason we permitted it to continue for as long as it did. Yet you surpassed all expectations. You uncovered truths no one else could. Truly, I should not be surprised. You are, after all, my sister." A flicker of pride passed across his eyes.

Her lips parted. "Who is 'we'? And what plan?"

He inclined his head. "There is an entire institution behind me, after all. It is an operation. We call it Operation Night."

"Operation Night." The words felt heavy on her tongue. She closed her eyes as understanding set in. She had been the bait, wriggling upon a hook.

"You knew what he was from the beginning," she said, after she opened her eyes. "T-Teddy." She struggled to pronounce the word. "All your talk of how elusive he was, how difficult to apprehend. Was that also false?"

"Not at all." Algie clasped his hands behind his back. "As I have said before, one cannot simply arrest Lucian Night. He must be caught in the act, with proof that is beyond dispute."

She remained rigid in her seat, her hands still tightly clasped. "You allowed him to court me. Yet you never intended for me to marry him."

He laughed shortly. "Most certainly not. The day before the wedding, at the latest, the entire matter would have concluded."

"Why me?" Her voice was barely audible. "Why involve me at all?"

"The idea came from Night himself. His creation of the Thaddaeus Linwood persona was designed to approach me through you. He believed that binding you to him would give him power. What he did not know was that we had seen through him from the start. We allowed it to continue, as it served our purposes. He believes he is in control. The truth is: we are." There was a quiet sense of victory in his tone, though Night had claimed precisely the opposite.

Isla picked up a small paperweight and turned it over in her hands. "And what will happen when you apprehend him?"

"He'll be tried at the Old Bailey. He'll most likely be sentenced to death."

She swallowed hard. "Could he not be transported? To Botany Bay, perhaps?"

"It is highly improbable. Not for a man of his record."

Lucian Night would hang. Teddy would hang. And she would be the one who had led him to the gallows. Not by mistake. Not by accident. She had played her part in full.

The sickness rose slowly within her.

It was justice. He had lied, deceived her, used her feelings for his own gain. He was a criminal. He deserved punishment.

And yet.

The weight of it was nearly unbearable.

"What now?" she asked, her voice scarcely above a whisper.

"The operation is nearly at an end. We intend to bring down Night and the entire Mudlark Skulls gang together. It must be done swiftly and cleanly."

"Swiftly and cleanly," she echoed, unable to summon any further reply.

"Yes." Algie rested one arm lightly on the back of her chair. His gaze was steady and clear. "But for it to succeed, we must ask you to continue your role. Just a little longer. Until the end. Do you understand?"

Isla looked up at him, her heart aching.

"Sometimes," she said quietly, "I believe I do not know you at all."

Chapter Nineteen

LADY ISLA WAS INDISPOSED.

This is what Falks, the butler, told any visitor with a mournful voice and a long-suffering expression. As a result, Isla received bouquets of flowers, well-wishes and concerned messages from all the visitors who had hoped to see her. Algie, too, had sent up a basket of oranges and a cordial of Dr Rothely's Purging Elixir, when she did not appear at breakfast the next morning.

It was entirely true. Isla lay in bed in a darkened room with a thudding headache. She had not slept a wink, but tossed and turned all night.

She was mourning Teddy.

Dear, sweet Teddy, who had turned out to be nothing but a fictitious creation, a charming illusion crafted by one of the most despicable men in London.

Teddy, who had claimed he loved her. Teddy, whom she had grown genuinely fond of and, in quiet moments, believed herself to be in love with as well.

Shy, sweet Teddy who would not harm a fly, who

read every wish from her eyes, whose greatest passion (besides courting her) was clocks.

Perhaps he would appear again that morning, waiting for her at the bottom of the staircase, a crooked smile on his face and a bouquet in his hand, and everything would be as it had been.

But no.

She need not ask why he had done it: that much was obvious.

Lucian Night had assumed the persona of Lord Thaddaeus Linwood to worm his way into her life and gain leverage over his arch-nemesis: her brother. It was a wicked, vicious plan, but also utterly brilliant. She had to grant him that.

Isla gazed sadly at the special orchids he had gone to such lengths to find for her. The story had been so charming, but it was more than likely it had never happened at all. The flowers stood in their pot on the table by the window and had wilted, clearly struggling in their current environment. She would instruct the maid to remove them.

What was she to do now?

They had both betrayed her, the two men she had loved most.

One had been her life, her family. Her trust and faith in Algie had always been absolute. There had never been a secret she had kept from him, a fear he had not eased, a doubt he had not assuaged. Algie was her anchor, steady, unwavering, reliable. Good-natured, kind Algie, who had rescued her from the orphanage and comforted her when she cried herself to sleep, aching for Jem. Algie, who had always stood by her. Algie, who believed she could do no wrong.

But tonight, she had glimpsed something new: a cold, calculating harshness. She had always known, deep down, that this aspect of him existed. He was a politician, after all, a most successful one, and power demanded a certain ruthlessness. But never had he revealed it to her, nor admitted so openly that he had used her for his own purposes.

A part of her comprehended why he had done it.

Lucian Night had presented him with an opportunity that was too good to refuse. Yet instead of including her openly in his schemes, Algie had chosen to leave her in the dark. He had said that Night was his marionette. Well, so was she. He had pulled the strings, and she had danced to his melody. Unwittingly, unknowingly, only to discover she'd been but a worm on a hook.

Fish bait.

It wounded her deeply.

She shivered, even though the fire blazed in the hearth, and she curled in the armchair, rubbing her arms in an attempt to console herself.

Then there was the other. Merely thinking about him caused a dull, throbbing ache in the area of her heart that nearly made her gasp.

If Algie's betrayal stung, this one made her bleed.

Algie, she could forgive. It would be difficult, but one day, she knew she would work through it all and reach that point when she could release her anger and absolve him.

But Teddy. How could she ever forgive him?

How could she ever forgive herself?

How was she to endure the next few days, knowing what she did now?

Algie wanted her to continue the charade until the bitter end. She would need to go on playing the role of the enamoured betrothed in public. She'd have to smile at Night, pretending she had not witnessed his crimes.

She would have to feign affection, allow him to hold her hand as though nothing had changed.

She jumped up from her armchair and walked up and down, agitated. What if he tried to embrace her? What if he, heaven forbid, attempted to kiss her again? Would she have to permit it?

Isla let her head fall against the back of the armchair with a groan.

It was so utterly vexing, this entire situation!

THE INSTRUCTIONS she'd received from Algie were clear. She was to maintain a cheerful, tranquil facade, eagerly anticipating her wedding.

"Continue with the activities as planned," Algie had advised. "Let him take you on walks in the park, to balls, dinners, and so forth. Use every acting skill you possess. Do not let him suspect that you know of his true identity. Do not address what you have witnessed at the warehouse. My advice is that you act as though that scene in the warehouse never happened. Erase it from your memory. It's the only way to remain convincing."

"What you're asking for is cruel," Isla whispered.

"I'm certain you can do this. Have faith. It won't be for long, I promise."

Now, as Isla prepared for their ride to Regent's Park, she steeled herself, determined to behave as if nothing had changed. She tied the bonnet under her chin more firmly than usual.

Teddy arrived in his curricle.

He looked splendid, dressed in grey, with a beaver hat sitting at a rakish angle. He jumped down with lithe grace and beamed at her when she stepped outside. It was jarring to see him like this, when her last memory of him was in that horrible warehouse, spitting out orders to his minions in that cold voice of his.

She repressed a shudder and squared her shoulders.

Act, she told herself. Act.

She forced a smile onto her face.

"Isla." He took her hand and kissed it. "I was terribly worried when I learned you were ill. Are you certain that you feel better now?" He looked at her with such earnestness that a lump stuck in her throat. His voice was affectionate and not at all cold and cruel.

"Certainly," she managed to say. "I am much improved. Getting some fresh air will be quite the thing as I've been languishing in my room for the past few days."

Her conversation felt stilted, but it was the best she could do for the moment.

He helped her into the curricle and tugged a woollen blanket about her with solicitous care.

"It is too warm for a blanket," Isla protested.

"We need to make sure that you won't fall ill again,"

he said, and would have tucked a heated brick under her feet if she hadn't protested vehemently that she would die of heat.

TEDDY CHATTERED CHEERFULLY about this and that, including the clock he'd espied in Lord Alfred Hambry's sitting room, quite by chance. "It is a real Tompion clock, Lala, one of the year-long clocks," he said, and proceeded to describe the longcase made of walnut, while Isla fiddled with the strings of her reticule, letting him talk. "I tried to talk him into selling it to me, but he refused. I might not have offered him enough of an incentive," he added in an afterthought. "I was thinking it would be the perfect clock for the corridor in our home."

Our home, he'd said. A touch of melancholy over-came her as she realised that would never happen.

"How many clocks will we have in our home?" she asked with a deliberately cheerful smile.

"At least twenty," he replied promptly, then proceeded to describe them all with such earnestness that she found it difficult to accept that he was pretending. His face was animated, his cheeks were covered with a faint flush, his brown eyes sparkled with enthusiasm.

Her gaze fixated on his lips, watching them move. His upper lip was fuller than the lower one, and the corners of his lips lifted upwards when he talked. His enthusiasm was infectious and charming. Surely, he couldn't be that good an actor to feign such sincerity.

"You don't happen to have a twin brother, do you?" she interrupted curtly.

He dropped the hand with which he attempted to indicate the size of the clock and gave her a startled look. "Not that I know of."

"Pity," she said under her breath.

Teddy parked the curricle under a tree by the boating lake. His tiger, John, jumped from his stand at the back of the curricle and retrieved a wicker basket.

"I thought we might take luncheon here," Teddy said, gesturing toward the lake, "since the weather is fine, and the view finer still."

The water lay still and glassy, disturbed only by the gentle drift of swans and ducks gliding between reeds. A soft mist rose in silver tendrils, lending the scene the dreamy quality of a Turner painting.

John spread a blanket beneath the shelter of trailing willows and unpacked their picnic: cold meats, a crusty loaf, ripe fruit, and a bottle of wine.

Isla felt her tension ease, caught up in the quiet romance of the moment. The crisp air sharpened her appetite, and she bit eagerly into a ruby-red strawberry.

"Food always tastes better out of doors," she said, reaching for another. "Twice as good, at least."

Teddy nodded, assembling a simple slice of bread with meat. "It doesn't need to be champagne and caviar. Sometimes the plainest fare outshines a king's banquet." He held the slice toward her. "Here—try."

She leaned forward and took a bite, her lips grazing his fingers. A blush bloomed in her cheeks. She touched her mouth, flustered, and turned her gaze to the lake.

There was something unexpectedly intimate in being fed.

Just when she wanted to turn to him to ask whether he could pour her another glass of wine, a girl stepped from the shadow of the tree.

"Would you have your fortune told, my lady?"

The voice was high and clear, and came from a bare-foot child in the bright, fluttering garb of the Rom. She could not have been more than seven, yet she held herself with the poise of a seasoned performer.

A second figure crept up behind her and clung to her side—a boy in tattered clothing, with wild, unkempt hair and eyes black as pitch.

Jem.

Isla gasped. Her hand flew to her throat.

But no, of course it wasn't Jem. It couldn't be. This boy was far younger, no more than five. And yet... the resemblance struck like a blow. That same narrow face, the pointed chin, the deep, watchful eyes that seemed to carry far too much sorrow for so small a frame. A gaze filled with hunger; not for food, but for something deeper, more elusive.

"Only a farthing," the boy said, stepping forward. He held out a grubby hand with a smile too practised for his years.

She knew the routine, of course. She had done the very same at that boy's age, with Jem at her side. While the girl spun tales of fame and fortune to distract the lady, the boy's quick fingers would go to work, slipping purses from pockets, unfastening watch chains, lifting silk hand-kerchiefs with practised ease. It was a performance Isla knew all too well, because once, she had played every part, despite Vanya's disapproval.

Despite knowing all that, she extended her hand. "By all means. I am curious to hear what fortune lies hidden in the lines of my palm."

The girl stepped up to her and took her hand in both of her own. Her fingers were small, cool, and smudged with dirt. Gently, she spread Isla's palm open and traced the lines with a fingertip as she spoke.

"Your mind is cleaved in two. The past and the present. What once was, what is, and what might yet return. Light and darkness. Trust and doubt. Courage or cowardice. Joy or fear. But be warned. You walk a knife's edge, swaying first one way, then the other. You can no longer afford to hesitate. You must choose. Take a stand. Show your colours. Will it be love, or will it be death? The choice is entirely in your hands."

Isla felt the blood drain from her face. It was as if an oracle had spoken. Every word rang true, echoing deep inside her.

"How...how did you know?"

The girl dropped her hand. "It is written in your palm."

Isla rubbed her hand against her side. She had never truly believed in palm reading, though Vanya had been quite good at it. To this day, she wasn't sure whether Vanya had made it all up or had genuinely seen people's fates in the curl of their fingers and the creases of their skin. But this girl, with her uncanny hazel eyes, seemed to see more than just lines.

Thus distracted, the boy went about his work.

"Oh no, you don't," Teddy exclaimed, spinning

around just in time to snatch the boy's wrist as it reached for his fob.

A hullabaloo erupted. John lunged forward with a shout—"Pickpocket!"—just as the boy yelped, caught in flagrante delicto. The girl burst into tears.

"Cal!" she sobbed.

And suddenly, it was all a perfect muddle.

Teddy had the boy nailed on the ground with one hand, and with the other, holding the girl.

The girl whispered something to the boy in Romani, "Kick him in the shins and then run," which Isla understood.

Teddy jumped out of the boy's path, so the boy kicked into empty air, and he tightened his grip on his neck instead. The boy wailed.

"There, there," Teddy said reassuringly, to calm the child down.

"I'll call the constable, my lord," John said, ready to scamper off. A constable would come and throw the two children into prison, where, no doubt, they would perish.

"No," Teddy said in a clipped voice, just as Isla was about to open her mouth to protest. To the boy, he said, "Cease struggling, boy. I will release you now, but if you run off, John here will go after you, capture you and clap you into gaol without a blink of an eye. But if you remain here quietly, no harm will befall you."

The boy stopped struggling and threw him a mistrustful look.

Teddy released him. "There. You see? Nothing will happen. And now, if you please, return my fob, my watch and my handkerchief." Teddy extended a hand. The boy squirmed, then reluctantly drew forth the demanded items and handed them to Teddy.

"I can't believe we fell prey to such a scheme," Isla sighed, shaking her head.

"He didn't mean it," the girl sobbed, "please do not punish him."

The boy burst out crying as well, and both stood in front of them, sobbing loudly.

Teddy shook his head, disconcerted. Then he handed his handkerchief to the girl, saying, "Here, wipe your face and blow your nose," which she did. When she returned the handkerchief to him in a soggy, wet ball, he waved it away. "Keep it."

Then he crouched down to be on the same level as the boy. "You know that stealing is not the way to succeed in life, don't you?"

Isla crossed her arms across her chest and raised an eyebrow.

The boy hiccupped.

"Crime is not the way to go," he lectured. "It will end you in gaol and before you know it, you're dangling and that's not a nice way to end one's life."

Isla choked, then coughed, then turned away, pretending to thump against her chest as if she'd swallowed the wrong way.

"But you know all that," Teddy continued. "Do you not?"

"We're hungry, sir," the boy mumbled. "What else are we to do?"

Teddy nodded. "Of course you are." He reached down to the blanket, where there were still the leftovers of their meal, and assembled a plate with cold meats, bread and fruit, and handed it to the child. Then he did the same for the girl.

Both children stared at him. "Go on, eat," he repeated, seeing them hesitate. "Finish the entire thing. I daresay we are done with luncheon, are we not, Isla?"

Isla opened her mouth, then closed it, then nodded.

They didn't need to be told twice. The children sat on the blanket and dug into their food as if there were no tomorrow.

While the children ate, Teddy polished his watch, for the boy's grubby hand had left fingerprints on it.

"How many handkerchiefs do you possess?" Isla said, after she had found her voice, for one must say something, and that was the only thing she could think of.

"Several." Teddy breathed on the clock and polished it meticulously, then lifted it to see whether it was clean. "One never knows when they may come in handy. I have one in each pocket, you see."

Certainly, on one hand it shouldn't surprise her, it occurred to her. His kindness towards social outcasts, particularly orphans. He was acquainted with children like them, after all. He must be familiar with poverty and hunger. When he had said that part about crime, she'd choked. The irony! But when she observed how kindly, how gently he interacted with these two children, she found it impossible to reconcile that this was the same person she'd seen three nights earlier, giving the cold-blooded order to exterminate a man.

She rubbed her eyebrow in confusion. It just did not add up.

After the children finished, he gave them a final lecture on righteous living, how they should never resort to lying, stealing and cheating, and how they should attend school, if at all possible.

The children nodded earnestly and promised.

Then, after pressing a coin into each of their hands, he sent them along their way.

Finally, he helped Isla back onto the curricle and set the cart in motion.

They rode in silence for a while. Then Teddy said, "I can hear your thoughts."

"Oh? What am I thinking, pray?"

"'He only helped those children to impress me,' is what you're thinking." She threw him a startled look. "It's true, is it not?"

"Partially," she admitted. "Most gentlemen would not trouble themselves with helping a pair of beggar children. Particularly if they are Gypsies."

"You have a fondness for them," he stated. "Because you spent some time with them."

She assented.

"You know what it is like to be that girl, to wander through the streets barefoot and hungry."

Once more, she assented.

"Do you want to tell me about that time?"

She did not, particularly, for he was Lucian Night, and surely, he must know what it was like to live in poverty, and to be hungry, for why else had he turned to crime to begin with? And he must be well acquainted with the Rom more than he let on. She was touched by the way he'd interacted with the children.

Thus, she said, "Yes, I am acquainted with hunger. It was our companion on the road." She suddenly saw a vision of Vanya in front of her, with her long, dark hair and her red skirt, her storm-grey eyes and her rough, calloused hands that gently plaited her hair.

"Don't steal," she'd admonished. "Never steal."

"But the one time we, that is, Jem and I, resorted to the same machinations as the pair we encountered—I would pretend to fortune read, mind you, a lot worse than the girl, while Jem filched their pockets—Jem's mum flogged our hides so we couldn't sit for three days." A smile flitted over her face as she remembered. "It is never all right to steal or to hurt someone. Even when you're hungry. Never." She looked straight into his eyes when she said it.

He returned her gaze, guileless, and innocent as a babe at dawn. "She must have been a truly remarkable woman," was all he said.

Chapter Twenty

Both Teddy and Algie were occupied the next day. Algie with his work, naturally, and Teddy with heaven knew what, possibly planning his next vile scheme. Yesterday's picnic had done nothing but confuse her further, for whenever Teddy was with her, there was nothing in his behaviour to suggest that he led a double life. What had astonished her most was how easily she had fallen back into their old conversational ease. For a short while, she had completely forgotten that he was Lucian Night. And when he attempted to kiss her goodbye while the butler was not looking, a quick peck on the cheek, she had allowed it.

It had felt natural.

Isla rubbed her cheek, troubled.

That day, Isla planned to visit Newgate Prison with Catherine and several other women from the 'Association for the Reformation of Female Prisoners'. They brought food and clothes to the inmates, as well as knitting and needlework, not only to provide occupation but also to calm them and help them earn a little money. It was no secret that the conditions at Newgate were appalling, and for women especially harsh. Thus, when Elizabeth Fry, who had founded the organisation, approached Isla for support, she had readily agreed.

The visit would keep her occupied and distract her from the troubling events of the past days and from Teddy.

Interestingly, the opposite occurred.

She spent the entire morning with the female prisoners, teaching one particularly young girl, only a few years older than the Romani girl from the day before, how to sew. As she departed, passing through the turnkey's room, Mrs Fry asked her to wait. She wished to speak with her after meeting with the warden. Isla and Catherine waited in the narrow chamber, where a grimy window overlooked a dark courtyard below. From there, they observed prisoners, both men and women, being moved between buildings.

"Mrs Fry is right," Catherine said, frowning at the sight. "Male and female inmates must be separated, urgently."

Isla watched a pair of men approach a woman who had just entered the yard. The woman looked about uneasily and shuffled into a corner. The men followed.

"Can't you stop them from harassing her?" Isla turned to the turnkey, who sat at a corner table, eating his dinner.

He shrugged. "There's naught I can do about it."

"But surely you must."

"As long as nothing's happenin', nothing's happenin'," he said, biting into a chunk of bread.

"There is clearly little interest in protecting the female inmates," Catherine said with a frown. "Mrs Fry is correct. We need reforms. A broader association, something nationwide, to raise awareness of this issue."

Isla was about to reply that this was precisely why they waited for Mrs Fry, when two turnkeys passed through the yard, dragging a prisoner between them.

She leaned closer to the windowpane, pressing her face against the glass.

That figure. Tall, lanky, wrists bound in iron cuffs, feet shackled by a short chain, in patchwork clothing, with a shock of unruly red hair.

"It cannot be," Isla whispered. Her eyes must be deceiving her. "How is this possible?"

It was the man Lucian Night had executed.

She had seen him die.

So why was he here, alive?

"Do you know him?" Catherine asked, her gaze shifting between Isla and the prisoner. "Who is he?"

The turnkey glanced outside. "That's Harkins. Right-hand man of the boss of the Mudlark Gang, he is. Nasty piece of work. They finally brought him in. Should've happened long ago. Set to swing tomorrow, I heard."

"But...but..." Isla pointed toward the man, unable to say she had seen him shot. "Who brought him in? And when?"

The turnkey shrugged. "'Bout three nights ago. Quiet-like. Heard it were some men from Bow Street, or someone even higher. Difficult to say. Whole thing stank of secrecy."

That was the night she had followed Teddy to the warehouse. The night she believed she saw the man shot.

But now the evidence proved otherwise. How could she have been so mistaken?

Her thoughts began to race. She had not truly seen him die, had she? She had turned away, hidden her face in her hands. She had heard the shot. But there had been no blood that she had noticed in the moonlight, and no body either. What if it had been a warning shot? What if they had taken him away?

"You said Bow Street men brought him in? Are you certain?" she asked sharply.

The turnkey paused with his bread halfway to his mouth and gave her a sidelong look. "I might be, and I might not."

"That means he knows something, if you pay him," Catherine murmured.

Isla took out her purse and handed him a coin.

He bit it, then pocketed it with a grunt of satisfaction. "Word is, there's a grand sweep happening. The government's taking action. That business with the Mudlark Skulls. Filthy trade, that one. They got wind of a shipment, or something worse. Three nights ago, they moved in, quiet as cats."

"And you're sure Bow Street brought him in?"

The turnkey leaned forward, lowered his voice. "That's the tale. But if you ask me? They weren't ordinary Runners. Too clean. Too sharp. I'd stake my wages they were government men. Secret sort. It's an open secret, miss—this town's crawling with them these days."

"Government men," Isla echoed. "You mean...agents from the Home Office?"

Algie.

The man shrugged. "More likely than not."

Isla's heart hammered in sharp staccato beats. Her mouth was dry, and she ran her tongue over her lips. "Lucian Night. What do you know about him?"

The turnkey gave another shrug. "Gone quiet, that one. No one knows where he is or what he is about. He's a phantom. Comes and goes like smoke."

Isla unclenched her fingers from her purse and slowly took out another coin. She pulled out another coin. "Thank you. That was most informative. Now, if you would be so good as to assist that woman in the court-yard, there's another coin in it for you."

The man's face lit up. "Certainly, my lady. No trouble whatsoever."

As the carriage rattled back toward Mayfair, Catherine cast a sidelong glance at Isla. "Would you care to tell me what that was about?"

Isla closed her eyes for a moment before replying. "I have a brilliant brother, Catherine. Truly."

Catherine chuckled. "I daresay we all know that."

"But there are moments," Isla said through gritted teeth, "when I could strangle him with my bare hands."

Catherine laughed again, but Isla only rubbed her temple.

She didn't know whether to laugh, weep with relief, or begin planning her brother's demise in earnest.

Instead, she let out a groan and banged her head softly against the side of the carriage, repeatedly.

"Isla!" Catherine exclaimed. "Whatever is the matter? Do you need some hartshorn?"

"I shall kill him," Isla muttered.

And Teddy with him.

Lucian Night.

A government man.

Why in heaven's name had she not realised it sooner?

Chapter Twenty-One

Isla's first impulse was to run to Algie, to demand the truth behind her suspicions. But something made her pause. No. She ought to speak to Teddy first. If anyone could explain the tangle of secrets, it was him. The question was...where to find him?

When she arrived home, the butler met her with a puzzled look and an enormous bouquet of blush pink roses and lily of the valley, tied with a navy ribbon.

"A boy delivered it, miss," he said. "Soot-streaked and breathless. Said he came from somewhere near Seven Dials, and that the gentleman told him not to tarry."

Isla's heart gave a small flutter.

Tucked between the flowers was a folded note in Teddy's familiar hand:

My DEAREST, *Alas, I am beset by obligations and cannot steal away, but let these roses stand in my place for now.*

Two more days, and I shall be entirely yours (provided you do not change your mind).

   Your devoted (and impatient) servant,
   T.

SHE STARED AT THE WORDS. Their wedding. In two days! She had entirely forgotten.

And yet—he had not.

Seven Dials. That was where the warehouse was.

If Teddy was anywhere in London, it was likely he was there, or at the gambling club.

She made her decision.

She would go to the warehouse. And this time, she would not leave with unanswered questions. She would confront him and get to the truth.

She rang the bell. "Tell Meggie to fetch her cloak. We are going out."

SHE FINALLY FOUND the warehouse after losing her way twice and doubling back through a warren of alleys and crooked streets. The air smelled of smoke, rotting fruit, and damp stone.

Meggie, who was usually at ease in the rough parts of town, glanced about nervously and pressed close to Isla. "I think we're being followed," she whispered to Isla.

Isla looked over her shoulder but found nothing unusual in the busy street. "Nonsense. Who should follow us, and why?"

"I don't know, m'lady, but it's a strange feeling I have."

Isla gripped her umbrella tightly. "Let them follow us. We're not doing anything wrong."

"This bit's worse than where we was before," she muttered. "If we get out o'here with all our teeth, it'll be a miracle."

"Never fear," Isla said, forcing a brightness she didn't feel. She raised her umbrella like a sword. "For I have my trusty weapon! My brother gave me a new one with a sharper tip."

Meggie snorted. "Aye, and we've all seen what *that's* worth. Don't go stabbin' at shadows, now."

They stopped in front of the door with green peeling paint and the red wolf sign painted upon it. Isla swallowed nervously. Then she pushed against the door, which creaked open under her touch.

The courtyard in plain daylight looked even more bleak than it had at night. As before, there was not a soul to be seen. She found that strange. Why were there no people guarding the place? They crossed through the courtyard and stopped before the door on the other side. Isla told Meggie to wait there. "If I am not back in fifteen minutes, run and fetch my brother."

The room that she had witnessed through the window, where she had seen Teddy—or rather, Lucian—in his element, was entirely bare. The chair and the table she had seen were gone.

The room was half in shadows.

Disappointed, her eyes swept through the room. There were not even so much as crates or barrels, nothing at all but the creaking wooden floor. Both sides of the room had windows, one facing the courtyard, where she had stood, and the other what she supposed must be another courtyard or street. She stepped further into the room to take a look, then paused.

There, in the shadows at the farthest end of the room, stood someone.

Her heart began to gallop.

There, with his back towards her, looking out of the window, was—

"Teddy," she gasped.

He turned around slowly.

"That—that—I—that is," she cleared her throat. "What are you doing here?" she blurted out, aware that it was an entirely nonsensical thing to say.

He regarded her, unsmiling. "You have a terrible sense of timing, my love."

She looked into his eyes, and they were as cold as a stranger's.

Isla gaped.

"Why the surprised look? I knew, of course, that eventually you'd put two and two together. I gather you already have, for you're far too intelligent not to. Though I imagine you talked yourself out of what your brain was telling you. Since you said nothing. Until now."

"Teddy," Isla repeated, unable to form any other word.

A door from the other end of the room opened, and armed men entered. They were a ragged group and looking very dangerous.

"Everything is ready, my lord. All the men are assembled," said one with a red bandanna over his head. His sleeves were rolled up and Isla saw the tattoo of a skull with two swords behind it. A pirate. The Mudlark Skulls. His eyes fell on Isla and stopped in his tracks. "But what is this?"

"A minor inconvenience," Lucian Night replied pleasantly. "You need not concern yourself with her."

Isla gasped.

Lucian turned to her, a flicker of regret in his eyes. "As I said, the timing is most unfortunate. A little later would have been preferable. We are in the middle of finalising a deal, you see. The Blood Wolves and the Mudlark Skulls are to be united under my leadership." He smiled in such a cold, calculating way that an icy shiver ran down her back. "Finally." He clasped his hands behind his back and strolled towards her. "I have achieved my goals, you see. Sole dominion over the underworld. Control over the Skulls. And my nemesis, the Home Secretary, dancing to my tune."

"I don't understand." Her voice shook. "I thought you worked with Algie, that you were one of his agents..."

He smiled. "Yes, that is what I wanted everyone to believe. It worked beautifully. But why give him such power when I can have it all?" He extended a hand. "With his sister in my grasp, he is but a marionette in my hands, a puppet I can crush at will. Alas, as I have said before, the timing of your discovery is deplorable. After the wedding would have been preferable," he mused. "At the very latest."

"Wedding?" She stared at him as if he'd gone mad.

"Well, yes. We are to marry, are we not?"

"You can't possibly believe I'll go through with it."

"Why not?" He smiled slowly. "I can't think of any obstacle in the way of our loving union, can you?"

"You're mad!" She gripped her umbrella. A man with a flintlock lunged forward—only to stop when Lucian raised a hand.

"Attention, all. She is mine. Anyone who touches her dies."

The men stepped back.

Somehow, that didn't comfort her in the least. Instead, anger surged through her.

She marched toward the door, where a heavy-set man blocked her path.

"Where are you going?" Lucian asked. "We haven't finished our conversation."

"I have. And I am going home to Algie." She whirled around and glared at him. "He'll have you, and this entire lot, arrested. You'll have to kill me to keep quiet."

"Will I?" He inspected his nails. "I have more subtle methods."

She froze. "What do you mean?"

He made a slight gesture, and one man scuttled forward with a chair.

"Please. Have a seat. Bring some tea too," he said.

The man brought a small table, and sure enough, began pouring piping hot tea from a teapot.

Isla pressed her hands to her hips to keep them from shaking. He was mad, completely mad, if he thought she'd sit and drink tea with him as if nothing at all were amiss.

"Sit," he said again, and this time his voice was sharp,

so sharp that she dropped into the chair without thinking, startled by the command.

"There. That's better." He poured her a cup and handed it to her. "Here. Drink. You're paler than a corpse. I don't want you toppling over."

He held the cup out to her.

"It's not poisoned," he added impatiently, then poured himself a cup and took an exaggerated sip, as if to prove his point.

She picked up the cup and took a cautious sip. The warmth spread through her limbs, loosening her joints and stirring her frozen thoughts. Her stunned mind functioned again.

Lucian watched with approval.

"There. Better, is it not? Now, let us continue our conversation. There are two matters to address. First, the wedding. Then, Algie."

He ticked off both points on his fingers.

"They are irrevocably related, of course. First, the wedding. We will proceed as planned."

"I'm the ultimate prize, of course," Isla said, staring hard into his eyes. "The sister of the Home Secretary. The ultimate coup."

She gave a harsh laugh.

He lifted a hand in acknowledgement. "I see we understand each other perfectly."

"Though how naïve do you think I am? That I would not tell him your secret? He will realise you have double-crossed him in no time."

"Of course you would tell him everything, and of

course he will realise it all. But you are naïve in thinking your brother didn't know about it all along."

Lucian took another sip of tea as Isla's world came crashing down.

"What do you mean?" she whispered. She set down her cup with a shaking hand.

"The entire thing was your brother's idea, of course." He gave a lazy shrug.

An icy chill spread through her chest.

"You lie."

"My dear Isla, I lie about many things, but not this. Your brother came to me, believe it or not, not to arrest me but to seek my help in rooting out the Rivergang Pirates, otherwise known as the Mudlark Skulls. Nasty lot. Now, I have my fingers in many pies, but this pie deals in a business even I find distasteful. Human trafficking." He pulled a face. "He begged me. The great and almighty Lord Algernon Wynthorpe. I was as astonished as you are now."

Lucian chuckled.

"You can imagine how much I relished the moment. I refused at first. Hold out my hand in peace to my arch nemesis? Never. But then, you see, he made me an offer. A delectable, irresistible offer."

He smiled in such a sinister way that Isla stared, aghast, unable to believe that the man who looked like her dear, sweet Teddy simply was not.

"He played his ultimate trump card." He lifted his hands. "I simply could not resist."

She had not imagined it. That night Algie and Lucian Night had held a conversation in the library.

Lucian truly had the upper hand over her brother.

A sick feeling punched her in the stomach.

"Yes. Algernon Wynthorpe sold off his sister to the Lord of the Underworld," Lucian said with another chuckle. "A brilliant move, really. He gets my help, and I get a lifelong warranty by becoming his brother-in-law."

"Never," she gasped.

"You may, of course, refuse to cooperate." He shrugged, utterly unbothered. "I cannot force you to marry me, after all. But then..." He leaned in, eyes glittering. "The agreement with your brother becomes void. And yet, I still hold the upper hand."

She clenched her fists. "How?"

"Through you, naturally. A most tempting hostage. Your brother would do anything for you, would he not?" Lucian gave a low, amused laugh. "Makes one wonder if the wedding is even necessary, now that you have followed me into my lair—willingly, I might add."

She stared at him, appalled.

"So, you see, my dearest love, your brother is clay in my hands. And I shall mould him to suit my purposes. Marry me, or do not. It hardly matters." He glanced into his teacup with feigned contemplation. "The choice is yours: this can be pleasant, or rather...unpleasant. For you. For him. And, perhaps, even for me," he added idly.

Her hands tightened until her knuckles turned white. "You are blackmailing me. If I don't marry you, my brother will pay the price."

"It is a bit of a pickle, is it not? The great Lord Algernon Wynthorpe, entangled with the underworld. Who would have guessed?" He leaned in, voice silken.

"Just imagine what they'll say: Parliament, society, the press. But it's not merely his reputation at stake. There's prosecution to consider. Newgate. Or worse." He rubbed his neck, mock thoughtful. "I cannot quite recall what they do with traitors these days. Hanging, drawing and quartering always had a certain flair. Though they might favour beheading now. Since hanging has proven itself to be rather unreliable. I speak from experience." He chuckled as if he'd made a joke.

Isla jumped to her feet. "They would not! You...you would not!" But even as she said those words, she knew that he very well might.

"Poor Isla. You should not have been so curious. You might have enjoyed a little more time in the blissful delusion of being betrothed to the dolt Linwood. Your brother has sold his soul to me. In for a penny, in for a pound. He has dug his own grave and from now on he will dance to my tune."

"You really are evil." Her voice shook.

"I see you finally behold my true nature."

More men pressed into the room. These were Lucian's own men, for she saw the wolf mark on them, and she lost count of how many. It was all lost.

Isla collapsed into her chair, drained of strength, on the verge of tears.

Lucian stepped forward. She snatched up her umbrella to jab him with it, but he leapt aside just in time.

"Oh no, you don't." He wrestled the umbrella from her grasp and tossed it away. He seized her and yanked her against his chest. She stared miserably into his face, which was Teddy's face, his eyes, his smile. No, not his smile. This one was sinister.

She shivered.

He pulled her closer. "Poor Isla. You must trust me now more than ever, my love," he murmured, his warm breath brushing her ears, making her shiver.

Just as she was about to look up and ask what he meant, the door opened, and pandemonium broke loose.

A group of armed men burst into the room. Lucian tightened his grip, flipped her around, and drew her further into the corner. It happened so quickly that she found herself in an iron hold from which she could not break free.

"Stop, in the name of the government. You are all under arrest," a voice rang out. There were more men than Mudlark Skulls in the room, and in the next moment a hullabaloo broke out. Shots fired, fists flew, bodies hit the ground, and Isla remained trapped in Lucian Night's grasp.

"Stop this instant," he bellowed, his icy voice slicing through the din. To her astonishment, the room fell still. She felt something cold press against her temple.

"Leave or she dies."

"Teddy," she gasped, hardly believing what she had just heard.

Then a figure stepped through the smoke and din with measured steps. Impeccably dressed and unruffled, he drew a flintlock from his coat.

"Wynthorpe. We meet again," Lucian said, his tone lightly amused.

"My lord," said an agent, his eyes darting to Isla. "We

have them under control, except for Night, who, as you see, has your sister."

"Step aside, Brown. You are in my way." Algie pointed his flintlock and aimed it straight at them.

"Algie," Isla breathed. If he pulled the trigger, and he only had that one shot, she was in the line of fire.

"Remind me again," Algie said, calmly closing one eye to aim, "what they call me?"

"Deathmark, my lord."

"And why?"

"Because you never miss."

Lucian laughed.

Algie fired.

Something zinged past the tip of Isla's left ear.

Lucian Night fell, laughter still curling on his lips, shot straight through the heart.

Chapter Twenty-Two

LORD ALGERNON WYNTHORPE WAS A HERO, the papers proclaimed.

He'd single-handedly brought down England's worst criminal, the Lord of the Underworld, the mastermind of crime. He had slipped through the fingers of justice for years, causing no end of trouble, even escaping the gallows. But no more. Thanks to Wynthorpe, the rookeries were cleared and both the notorious Mudlark Skulls and the fearsome Blood Wolves, two of the most feared crime syndicates that had ever terrorised the streets of London, had been apprehended. 'The streets of London are safe once more,' the papers declared, 'thanks to the decisive actions of Lord Wynthorpe.'

In parliament, the House members cried "hear, hear" so thunderously the walls trembled, and men on the streets tossed their hats in the air when they saw him pass by.

The Duke of Wellington, the hero of Waterloo, invited him to a gala supper at his residency, 'Number

One, London,' Apsley House. People soon referred to the event as 'The Supper of Heroes.'

"From one hero to another," Wellington told Algie suavely, clapping him on his shoulder, "let me confess that heroism is a heavy burden which is best borne in the company of those who understand it."

Isla had been invited to attend, but she declined, citing a splitting headache. That was not untrue; but the real reason was not one she could publicly share. The day had been intended for her wedding, and she could not, would not, face society with a smile. No one knew that her betrothed, Lord Thaddaeus Linwood, was in truth Lucian Night. It was a secret that would remain forever buried. Algie had suggested they claim the wedding had merely been postponed, and that Linwood had embarked on an urgent voyage to the Indies due to family reasons, never to return.

"He won't be returning from the trip, as his ship will sink. It is the cleanest way to rid ourselves of him," he had said curtly.

She had scarcely recognised her brother at that moment. His voice had been cool and precise, as though he were closing a ledger rather than disposing of a man's life. Isla had said nothing, only looked at him with wide, sorrowful eyes.

But to Catherine, she'd poured out her heart.

"It is a strange thing," she told her, when Catherine stopped by briefly on her way to Apsley House, "A widow is permitted to grieve her husband. But when a wedding ends before it begins, because the bridegroom is unmasked as a criminal, and then dies, shot by her own brother, the bride is left in an odd kind of limbo. There is no name for what she is. I cannot even wear mourning. It would be considered improper."

Catherine teared up. "Oh, Isla," she whispered and gathered her into her arms.

Yet Isla, curiously, had not cried.

She found herself unable to.

"The worst thing," she murmured into Catherine's shoulder, "is that the brother I have loved, adored, admired, and trusted all my life has become someone I barely recognise. Perhaps it is a sign I never truly knew him at all. There is a side to him he never showed me. Brilliant, yes. But manipulative. Successful, yet utterly ruthless. He pulled the trigger and ended a man's life without hesitation, without remorse." Her voice faltered. She paused, swallowed, and pressed on. "It is a side I cannot abide. I find myself beginning to dislike my own brother. I no longer trust him. He feels like a stranger. There. I have said it."

Isla sniffed and gently withdrew from Catherine's embrace to search for a handkerchief.

"Oh, Isla," Catherine said again, her eyes troubled. "It is no wonder you feel this way. You must feel terribly used, as though he trampled your feelings in pursuit of his own aims. Forgive me for saying so, but I see it from the outside perspective as well. Every decision he made was in service of the Home Office. Your happiness was sacrificed for what he believed to be the greater good. I do not say this to excuse him. You have every right to feel betrayed."

"He used me. Lied to me. Not once, not twice, but

time and again." Isla pressed her fingers to her temple. "Perhaps it was for king and country, or whatever noble cause he deems worthy. But still." She gave a helpless shrug. "I was nothing but a pawn in a game I did not even know I was playing. He is my brother. Or... I thought he was. I suppose I shall call him Wynthorpe from now on. Algie is gone. I do not know who he is to me anymore."

"And Linwood?" Catherine's voice was quiet, full of concern. "You loved him dearly, did you not? And I mean Teddy, not Lucian Night."

A shadow crossed Isla's face. At the mention of his name, a dark wave of grief rose so forcefully that it left her gasping. With all the strength she could muster, she shoved her emotions back where they came from, that treacherous box of her heart, slammed the lid shut, and swallowed the wail rising in her throat.

"Love," she said with a brittle smile. "What is that? He said he loved me. And it was all a lie, spoken by a black-hearted criminal. He never meant a word. Yes, he deserved to die." Her voice wavered again. "If only for lying to me like that."

Catherine said nothing, but her eyes brimmed with sorrow. She patted Isla's hand gently. "You should rest, dear friend. Forgive the platitude, but time will heal all wounds."

Isla gave a hollow laugh. "And yet, despite everything, you rather like Wynthorpe, do you not?"

A faint blush crept into Catherine's cheeks. "He asked me to accompany him to the supper at Apsley House."

"That is tantamount to an official declaration of engagement." Isla waved a hand. "My felicitations."

Catherine plucked absently at a flower petal from the arrangement on the table. "He has not proposed. I hardly think a supper invitation constitutes an engagement."

Isla chuckled tiredly. "He is ruthless in matters of state, but when it comes to affairs of the heart, he turns lily-livered. My advice, Catherine: do not make it easy for him. If he wants to win you, make him beg. Let him crawl. Let him humiliate himself for love, publicly."

"Yes, yes," Catherine replied, still patting Isla's hand as though humouring a wilful child, her brow furrowed. "You really must rest now. I shall return tomorrow and tell you all about the gala supper."

For once, Isla did not mind being sent to bed.

Weeks passed. And Isla found herself in a strange, suspended sort of life. Her days unfolded just as they had before she ever met Teddy. She visited hospitals, orphanages, prisons, and charitable events. Her time was fully occupied, and each night she fell into a deep, dreamless sleep.

Only once did she dream. And vividly.

She dreamed of Vanya and of Jem.

Vanya, whose soft hands braided her hair while she sang a lullaby in that gentle, lilting voice Isla remembered so well. Vanya, who tucked her into a coarse woollen blanket as they lay beside the fire, sleeping on the bare ground. She saw the moors again and felt that aching loneliness rise in her chest, just as it had when she once ran barefoot over gorse and heather, calling out for Vanya. But Vanya was gone, slipping from her grasp like mist. Try as she might, Isla could not hold on to her.

She cried out, and sorrow swept through her. But someone else was there, gripping her hand.

Jem.

Jem, just as he had been at thirteen years old, with wild, thick, tawny hair and thin, lanky limbs. That ever-present whistle on his lips. Jem, who could flip coins in the air and make them disappear. Always a step behind her. Always there. Teasing her, shielding her, holding her hand. Jem, who had sat beside her at the orphanage. Jem, who was there when the grand carriage arrived from London, bearing the Wynthorpe crest. A beautiful lady had stepped down, Lady Wynthorpe, and beside her, a gentleman, Lord Algernon Wynthorpe. They had come to take Isla into a new world.

Jem had told her to go.

"I do not want to go," she cried.

"You must. You belong with them," he had said then, just as he said now, in the dream. "You must go with them."

"I do not want to go." Isla clung to him, weeping. Over and over, she cried. "I do not want to go." But Jem gently uncurled her fingers from his hand. She tried to hold on, but he slipped from her grasp. Then, like Vanya, he began to rise, higher and higher, until he vanished into the sky.

Meggie woke her.

"M'lady, wake up now. Come on, wake up." She was shaking her gently.

"Meggie?" Isla blinked at her, dazed.

"There now, there," Meggie murmured, patting her arm. "Ye don't have to go. No one's forcin' ye. Ye don't have to go nowhere ye don't want to."

"I had a nightmare."

"Aye, that ye did. And a bad one too. Ye was thrashin' and cryin' in yer sleep, sayin' ye don't want to go—to that supper, I reckon, but ye ain't goin', over my dead body." Meggie shook out the blanket and tucked it round her. "I've never seen ye in such a state."

"It was only a dream." Isla wiped her cheeks. "Only a dream," she whispered.

But why, even in her dream, why had Jem told her to go? As if he had wanted to be rid of her. Why couldn't it have been different? Why couldn't she have dreamed he asked her to stay, just once? Not even in her dreams did the people she loved choose her. Not even in her dream did the people she loved stay by her side. The thought filled her with a deep bitterness.

JEM.

Thanks to that wretched dream, Isla's thoughts were full of him that morning. The boy she had loved so dearly, who had grown into someone she hardly recognised. She played with the thought of contacting him once more. She had not heard from him since that strange meeting at the inn. She had not reached out to him, and clearly, he had not cared to send a note either. He must know where to find her. After all, she was the sister of Wynthorpe.

She picked at her breakfast with little appetite. These days she took her meals in her own morning room, no longer in the dining room with Wynthorpe. They no longer shared luncheons or suppers either. In truth, she rarely saw him now. Which was just as well.

He had buried himself in work.

"Did you turn him down?" Isla asked Catherine once, wondering whether his increased workload was an attempt at healing a bruised heart.

"How could I turn him down when he never proposed?" Catherine replied dryly. "I confess I grow weary of waiting, Isla. He cannot feel too deeply if he cannot even be bothered to ask for my hand." She shrugged. "I have other suitors too, you know."

Isla nodded. "Perhaps it is for the best. Wynthorpe is the sort of man who will always be married to his work. You deserve better."

Chapter Twenty-Three

Summer had given way to a cold and blustery autumn, with an early snowfall. The weather suited Isla's current mood. Three months had passed, and still she had not forgiven her brother.

She feared she never might.

At one point, Isla cautiously made inquiries about where Teddy might have been buried. She had a quiet yearning to visit his grave, just once. But she could not bring herself to ask Wynthorpe. Instead, she asked Meggie to look into it discreetly, with the aid of a generous bribe to ensure silence.

"Well, m'lady, seems there was a bit of a muddle," Meggie reported. "They say 'e might've been taken to Potter's Fields. Or handed over to the college of surgeons. What with all of them bodies in the warehouse, they piled 'em into carts and mixed some of 'em up. Could be 'e was cut up first, and what was left buried in unconsecrated ground."

Her descriptions turned rather more graphic than

Isla cared to hear, and her face paled. "Thank you, Meggie. That was rather more detail than I required."

Even so, she went to Potter's Fields and laid a small bouquet on a pauper's grave. But her heart had felt empty, and her eyes had been dry.

Isla was taking breakfast in her morning room, alone, but she had little appetite. She toyed with her eggs, which had grown cold, and crumbled her bread roll to pieces.

Falks, the butler, suddenly appeared before her, making her jump. "Falks. I did not hear you come in."

"I beg your pardon, ma'am. His lordship is enquiring whether you might object to him joining you for breakfast."

"Wynthorpe hasn't left for work yet?" That was a divergence from his usual daily routine, for she was breakfasting late this morning.

"No, ma'am."

Isla shrugged. "Fine. He can join me if he wants. I have nearly finished my breakfast, however."

Algie hesitated in the doorway so that she didn't immediately see him. Isla set down her fork. "Good morning."

Algie cleared his throat. "Good morning. I only wanted to see how you are. Haven't seen you in a while. Been so busy lately."

"I'm well," Isla said evenly.

"Good. That is good to hear."

"Please, sit." They were speaking like strangers.

Algie sat. Falks brought a tray with coffee and toast and nothing more.

Isla raised an eyebrow. "That isn't your usual fare of beef, potatoes and French beans?"

"I find it necessary to lose some pounds," he replied. "The doctor prescribed a strict diet."

She set down her coffee cup. "Ah." Now that he mentioned it, he did seem to look somewhat trimmer, and his face had lost some of its roundness. It suited him.

"Otherwise, I'm in good health, in case you were wondering."

She nodded politely. Once, she would have fussed over his health and seen to his diet herself. Now she had not even known the doctor had called. It was a sign of how far apart they'd grown.

"You don't look too well yourself," he added with a worried frown. "You seem thinner, too."

They ate in awkward silence, with Isla merely pushing her eggs from one side of the plate to the other.

Algie finally set down his cutlery and sighed. "Pixiekins."

She picked up her cup again, even though it was empty. "Hm?"

"When will you finally forgive me?"

His eyes were sorrowful.

Isla stared at her plate.

Forgiveness.

That wasn't something one could simply offer like that. She was hurting too much still. The pain was still too sharp. But neither did she want to go on like this, estranged from Algie. It was unbearable.

"There is no name on his grave," she said suddenly. "There is a simple cross, set there by some kind soul. But otherwise, only wild gorse and thistle and nettles grow there. Sometimes a dandelion or ragwort. I therefore took the orchid he once gave me. It will probably not survive in such a place, but I thought it was too sad that his grave should have no flowers at all."

Algie shifted around uncomfortably in his chair. "That is very thoughtful of you."

"Is it? I have done a great deal of thinking these past weeks. I have done nothing but think."

"What have you been thinking?"

She met his gaze at last, direct and unflinching. "The thought that haunts me the most is a question. A 'what if?'."

Algie shook his head. "Really, Isla, there is no point in dwelling on the past and on breaking one's head over 'what ifs' and to recriminate oneself over decisions that one has made. There is no sense in torturing yourself with what might have been. Whatever choice you made, there would only ever have been one outcome for Lucian Night. It was always going to end that way. In truth, this may have been a kinder, more merciful end. No trial, no spectacle, no scaffold. Surely you can see that?"

"I wasn't speaking about Lucian Night."

He gave a brief shake of his head. "Then of whom, pray, were you speaking?"

"Myself. I was thinking: What if I had refused to go with you and Mama at the orphanage that day? What if I had refused to listen to Jem and ran away, back to Lazlo's *kumpania*? Would my life not have been so very different? I would not have lost Jem. I would never have

242

known, and lost, Teddy." Her voice caught. She would also never have known Algie.

That realisation struck him as well. He stared at her, stunned. "Isla! You can't possibly mean that."

Didn't she? At that moment, she felt like she did. Very much so.

"You asked about what thoughts were going through my mind, and I have told you. Make of them what you will. I am, as you can see, not entirely myself these days." She pushed her plate back. "I have an appointment with Mrs Fry. If you will excuse me, I must get ready." She rose and left the room, casting a glance over her shoulder. Algie still sat at the table, as motionless as a marble statue.

THAT EVENING, he summoned her to his study. Isla, who had had a busy day, had planned on retiring early, but Falks appeared with a message from her brother, saying he wished to see her without delay.

"Immediately, he said?" She raised an eyebrow.

"Indeed, my lady. "

Algie stood in front of the fireplace, staring into the roaring flames.

"You wished to see me?" She folded her hands before her, feeling like one of the supplicants who visited his office each day.

Algie turned. "Indeed. Please. Do sit." He indicated the armchair by the fire, and she took her seat, smoothing her woollen skirt.

He came straight to the point. "I have spent the entire day thinking about what you said at breakfast. I have made the momentous decision to breach certain security protocols and tell you things I ought not to. Given the circumstances, I believe it is justified. I want you to know the truth, and I trust that nothing I am about to say will leave this room."

"By all means," she said quietly.

He took a brief turn about the room before continuing. "You must understand that secrecy is of utmost importance in order for these operations to work. It is upon which everything rests. Due to the nature of our operations, we often rely on agents and civilians to help us infiltrate parts of society that would otherwise remain closed to us."

Isla nodded. She had, after all, once assumed that Teddy had been such an agent.

"At times, we ask them to play certain roles to gather intelligence."

"Espionage," she said.

"Of sorts."

"Go on."

"Most times, this is not a problem. The difficulty we encountered with you was that your quick mind made you unusually adept at piecing things together."

Isla tilted her head. "Meaning?"

"Meaning that your investigations into Jem repeatedly interfered with our work."

She blinked. "I do not quite see how that could have been the case, but continue."

"There were several incidents where we had to delay our plans because of your presence. You decided to scour the rookery. You discovered the significance of the wolf insignia. You began searching for Lucian Night yourself."

Perhaps he had a point.

"Most significantly, where Jem Fawe was concerned, we decided, or rather I decided, to put an end to it once and for all."

She stared at him, uncomprehending.

"I hired someone to play the part." He paused, then continued. "I know this will do nothing to redeem me in your eyes. If anything, it adds to the wrongs I have already committed. But we needed you to stop looking for Jem Fawe."

"In other words, the man I met at the inn was not Jem at all." Her breath caught. Of course. A part of her had always known. He had seemed so distant. So utterly disconnected.

"But he knew things about our childhood that only Jem could have known."

Algie nodded. "That is because you did know him as a child. He was at the orphanage, too. He knew both you and Jem. His real name is Cam Lowe. He was also Romani."

"Cam Lowe." The name stirred something. An image surfaced of a scruffy boy trailing after Jem. He'd been younger, with perpetually hungry eyes, and a cruel streak. He was one of the mean boys who used to force her to give up her morning porridge. Until Jem discovered it one day, and smashed his fist into his nose, saying if he ever came near Isla again, he'd do worse. Cam had backed off after that, and Isla had completely forgotten about him.

Isla gasped. "You hired Cam to pretend to be Jem?"

"Yes."

"How could you?" she whispered.

His shoulders sagged. "I know it was a reprehensible thing to do. We were running out of time. I will not ask for your forgiveness. It is beyond forgiveness. But Isla, I want to make it right. And I have good news. I have found Jem. The real Jem. I want you to meet him. We can leave for Yorkshire tomorrow if you wish. If there is anyone who can help ease the pain you are feeling now, I believe it is him."

Chapter Twenty-Four

THE CARRIAGE SPED through the hilly landscape.

Isla had slept for several hours, but now she was awake, her head resting against the window as she pretended otherwise.

Algie sat opposite her, arms crossed, gazing pensively out into the passing scenery. Catherine, seated beside Isla, appeared to be asleep as well. Isla had insisted on bringing her, not because propriety demanded it, but more for emotional support. The thought of spending the entire journey alone with Algie had been intolerable. They had exchanged only the most superficial pleasantries. Isla suspected the journey was no more comfortable for Catherine, who remained caught in the unspoken possibility of a relationship that had once hovered between her and Algie. The status quo between them now was uncertain. Isla no longer cared. She had resolved to stop playing intermediary between them. Still, for this one trip, she had wanted Catherine close.

She felt utterly spent. Weary in both body and spirit.

And now she was about to meet Jem.

The real Jem. The boy she had spent years chasing through memories and shadows. She searched her heart and found only a flicker of curiosity. The urgency, the longing, the passionate obsession to find him that had once consumed her was gone.

Why should this meeting be any different from the last?

True, that time, she had met Cam, not Jem, though she had not known it then. A boy from the orphanage she barely recalled. That meeting, too, had been a lesson. A warning. The years had passed. Time had done its quiet work on them both. Their relationship had changed, as had their personalities.

He was no longer the boy she remembered.

Neither was she the timid little girl who'd used to trail behind him, like a puppy.

They had been so very young, so very naïve. Surely, life had hardened him too, and he must have become more cynical, more world-weary.

So now she travelled northward, not with anticipation, but almost with reluctance and a profound scepticism.

"We will arrive shortly." Algie sat up and straightened his hat.

She gave no reply.

"I know you are not sleeping, Pixiekins," he added after a moment. "You might as well look out. The landscape is worth admiring."

Her eyes fluttered open despite herself. Snow dusted the rolling hills like icing sugar. They were nearing the coast. She could smell the ocean. On a rise ahead sat a manor house, charming, modest, and elegant in its simplicity. Not too grand, not too small. From this distance, it looked like a doll's house, poised above the countryside, watching.

Something twisted inside her.

Teddy had once described a house just like this. He must have invented it, or perhaps he had not. Perhaps he had modelled it on this very place. For she recognised it.

And that hurt more than she had expected.

The coach turned and rumbled up a narrow lane flanked by leafless trees, leading to a large, forbidding grey stone mansion. A shiver ran through Isla as an eerie sense of familiarity stole over her. The surrounding park, the stark bleakness of the grounds; she knew this place.

Goosebumps prickled along her arms.

"Surely," she whispered, "this isn't Thornyhill Orphanage?"

She didn't need Algie's confirmation. She knew. She had last seen it on the day Algie and Mama came to take her away. Jem had run after the carriage, down this very lane, crying her name.

She'd heard his cry ever since in nightmares that plagued her to this very day.

The coach drew to a halt in front of the house. Isla stepped down as if in a dream, as though she had slipped backwards in time.

But it was not the stern matron of her childhood who emerged from the doorway, not the sharp-eyed woman with the grey bun and joyless voice, but a younger woman with kind features and a gentle smile.

"Welcome to Rosehill Orphanage," she said warmly. "I'm Mrs Anne Gardener, the matron and headmistress. It is always a joy to welcome back our former wards."

Isla took her hand with a dazed expression. "Rosehill? I remember it as Thornyhill."

"It was," Mrs Gardener replied. "The name changed after we acquired new patrons." She glanced meaningfully at Algie. "Thanks to their generous support, we were able to renovate the building extensively and make it far more welcoming. We added new windows, an entire additional wing, and modern furnishings."

She remembered the darkness, the cold, the nights shivering in shared beds for lack of enough linens or space.

Though the stone façade remained unchanged, Isla now noticed cheerful curtains in the windows. Inside, carpets softened the floor, and daylight streamed through widened panes. It was still the same place and yet utterly transformed.

Mrs Gardener ushered them into a sitting room and served tea.

"What wonderful changes," Isla murmured, wonder lacing her voice. Then she turned to Algie. "Is this your doing? Are you the new patron?"

"Mama was. I took over after her passing." He hesitated, then added, "I helped fund the renovations. But the real credit belongs to someone else. The estate had been sold some years ago, and the new owner took an interest in restoring it. I supported where I could, as Mama would have wished."

"We are deeply grateful for that support," Mrs

Gardener said. "We've hired more staff, and I daresay the children have never been happier."

Just then, a line of neatly dressed children passed on the staircase, their chatter light and cheerful.

"I can see that," Isla said softly. She had never wished to return. Too many painful memories, too many unanswered questions about Jem. Her enquiries had led nowhere, and she had seen no reason to revisit sorrow. But now, seeing the home in such capable hands, she was glad she had come.

"You did well," she said, at last looking her brother full in the face.

Algie cleared his throat. "Yes, well. I am neither the main patron nor the owner of this place."

"Owner?" she echoed. "I thought this was a parish-run institution, overseen by a board of trustees."

"It was. But about a decade ago, it was purchased outright, house, land, and all. It is now privately owned and operated," Mrs Gardener put in.

Isla stared at Algie. "You bought it?"

He waved a hand. "Not I. That honour belongs to someone else. In fact, it is him I brought you here to meet."

A wave of unease rose in her chest. She stood abruptly, knocking her teacup against the table so that the last of the tea sloshed over the rim.

"Then let us meet him now."

Algie chose to remain in the drawing room to speak with Mrs Gardener. Catherine elected to stay as well, wanting to learn more about the history of the place.

A maid led Isla through the main hall, across the

house, and out a glass door onto the back terrace, where several stone amphorae stood atop the balustrade, lending an air of bygone grandeur ill-suited for an orphanage. A wide flight of steps descended to a sweeping garden, now bare and dusted with snow.

The maid curtsied and withdrew, leaving Isla alone on the terrace. She glanced around with a faint frown and nearly missed the still figure beside one of the stone amphorae in the far-left corner.

Her heart pounded. Clad in sombre grey, he blended into the shadow, his back to her, leaning against the balustrade as he gazed pensively over the garden.

Isla trembled. She stopped two paces behind him, pressing her hands together to still their shaking. Her lips parted once, then again. Nothing came. She swallowed.

"It cannot be," she whispered at last.

He turned slowly, his expression unreadable.

"Well met, Lala," he said after a pause.

A rushing filled her ears. Her vision blurred, and sudden light-headedness caused her to sway.

Teddy sprang forward, catching her arm just as her legs threatened to give way. He guided her carefully to a stone bench by the wall and helped her sit, then remained standing over her, his brow furrowed with concern.

"This must be a dreadful shock," he said in a voice all too familiar. "I wish there had been a gentler way to tell you. I was against it from the beginning, but your brother, plague take him, insisted—" He broke off, his frown deepening, and knelt before her so they were face to face.

Reaching for her reticule, he opened it and rummaged inside.

"Ladies usually carry hartshorn salts...ah, here we are." He drew out the small silver vial, uncorked it, and held it beneath her nose.

The sharp, pungent scent stung her senses, and she jerked her head back in disgust.

"Ah. It works," he said dryly.

She stared into his deep brown eyes.

"But...why?" she whispered. "How? I saw Algie shoot you. There was blood...so much blood."

The furrow between his brows eased, and his expression turned rueful.

"A pig's bladder filled with blood, sewn beneath my coat. The ball was made of wax and fired with a reduced charge, just strong enough to rupture the pouch, but not enough to do actual harm. I wore a quilted waistcoat with a bit of steel reinforcement beneath. None of it was real."

"I don't understand." She shook her head.

"Lucian Night had to vanish. His part was played, and he was no longer needed." He rose and sat beside her, taking her hands in his. "Your hands are freezing." He began rubbing them between his own.

"Lucian Night was no longer needed." Isla repeated the words faintly, her mind struggling to keep pace. She pulled her hands away.

He huffed. "You have a knack for appearing at the worst possible moment. We were just about to bring the entire operation to a close. We had finally managed to gather every last member of the Mudlark Skulls and the Blood Wolves in one place. It would've been a clean, swift operation. The house was surrounded. All Algie and his men had to do was move in and take them." He shook his head. "Then the door opened. And who should walk in, bright and cheerful, and entirely unaware? You. We couldn't stop; we had to go on. You became a witness to the whole affair. It wasn't what we planned. Teddy was supposed to come to you that very afternoon, courting, roses in hand. It was all meant to be explained and revealed gently, with time. But once you saw Lucian die, things became complicated. Teddy had to vanish, too. Algie had him sent to the West Indies." He lifted his shoulders in a small shrug, then met her gaze with solemnity. "I regret how that had to be played out. I am sorry for the pain it must have caused. I wish there had been a way to spare you that pain."

"Pain," Isla echoed. She stared at him as though seeing him for the first time. "You mean to say it was all a performance? A charade? Something out of a play?" Her hand rose, pointing towards the house. "Planned by you and my brother?"

"It is a long story," he said softly.

"And Lucian Night?"

"A fabrication. A name I adopted. A role I played. I am an agent of the Home Office, Isla. It was my duty to infiltrate the underworld, and to do so, I had to become Lucian Night. All the crime, the human trafficking, it was all growing beyond our control. Severe and radical measures had to be taken. The entire operation was sanctioned and orchestrated by the Crown."

Her head spun once more. She closed her eyes and pressed a trembling hand to her temple.

"Stop," she whispered. She shook her head. "Are you telling me that Algie planned this? That he made you do it?"

"Correct. He has trained me for this for years. Decades, even. By becoming a crime lord, I became the Home Office's most effective weapon. I was not only at the very heart of the underworld, but its purported leader. I had access to everyone and everything and organised it all under the guise of leadership. Then I passed all the information on, naturally, straight to Algie."

Isla's mouth dropped.

"You may have wondered why Algie never moved against Lucian Night. That was because Lucian was never truly his enemy, but his accomplice. And it succeeded admirably. Thanks to your brother, we rounded them up and cleansed the rookery. Your brother is the mastermind behind all this. He truly has a brilliant mind."

Isla stared at him in disbelief. "Algie came up with all this. It had been planned for years, if not decades," she repeated.

"Yes."

"And then, when you didn't need Lucian Night anymore, he had to be disposed of in that dramatic manner, in front of as many witnesses as possible."

"We had not counted on you being there," he said apologetically. "We never intended to deceive you. You were never to know. But once you saw Lucian Night die, he had to remain dead. This meant that Lord Linwood had to go as well." He pulled a hand through his hair.

Isla gathered all the strength that remained in her to ask the ultimate question that burned most urgently in her soul. "And Lord Thaddaeus Linwood? Was he a fabrication as well?"

He cleared his throat. "That is indeed my name. It is the name my father gave me at my birth. He and my mother ran away together, but Vanya did not care to adapt to a conventional, settled way of life. She tried, but she was deeply unhappy, especially after she realised the marriage was a mistake. One day, she took me, and we returned to her family. There, she gave me another name."

The trembling took over her again, but she pulled herself together, upright.

"Jem Fawe." Her voice sounded indifferent, almost cold.

Their eyes met.

He gave an almost imperceptible nod. "Yes."

Chapter Twenty-Five

Isla jumped up from the bench, grabbed her umbrella, and pointed it at Teddy like a rapier. "Explain yourself."

He backed away, raising both hands in protest. "Careful with the umbrella, you're about to poke my eyes out."

"That is entirely intentional." She glared down at him. "Well?"

"It isn't as you think..."

She took another step forward, and the tip of the umbrella pressed into his chest.

"It's a rather long story."

"That we'd best be telling together, I suppose." Algie had stepped out onto the veranda. "It's all my fault, Pixiekins. No need to skewer him for it."

Isla scowled at him. "I fail to see how this isn't his fault."

Catherine stepped out behind him, her eyes bright with curiosity, coming to a sudden halt when she beheld Teddy. "Ooh! Linwood! Aren't you supposed to be dead and buried? I can't seem to decide whether you're a fiend or a friend. How vexatious of you. But wait—hold with the storytelling for one moment. Isla, dear, why don't we all gather inside, since it's freezing out here? Mrs Gardener is offering us some hot negus. Then, let us listen to his story, and I shall serve as your juror. If his tale isn't convincing, you may wallop him with your umbrella afterwards."

With her words, an icy blast of wind rose, and Isla shivered. She lowered her umbrella. "Very well. But take heed. If you utter another falsehood, I shall return to London at once and never talk to either of you again." She pointed her umbrella at Algie this time. "I shall disown you entirely and no longer call you brother. Mark my words. Come, Catherine." She took her friend's arm and sailed past Algie.

Algie rubbed his chin. "You had best make a decent job of it," he muttered to Teddy.

It was indeed more pleasant inside. The fire was roaring in the fireplace, and the maid had brought in a tray with mugs and hot negus. Mrs Gardener had excused herself, for she needed to tend to her wards.

Isla sat in an armchair by the fireplace, with Catherine next to her. Algie sat uncomfortably in a plain chair, and Teddy paced in front of the fire, pulling his hand repeatedly through his hair. When the maid offered him a mug, he declined.

Isla warmed her hands on the mug and sipped from it. The hot liquid spread through her, and she felt how it gave her fortitude. She was no longer frozen and shocked.

But furious.

The deception involving Lucian Night she could forgive. She could understand the reasoning behind it, could see how certain forces had converged to place her in the situation she now faced. And behind it all, she could see Algie's hand. But that he was Jem? All this time?

She narrowed her eyes at Teddy, who looked at her ruefully.

After the maid left, she set down her mug and crossed her arms. "Begin."

"Yes. Well. The thing is this. It is all rather complicated. Where to start? The story is somewhat convoluted—"

"You're not helping your case," Algie growled.

"Starting at the beginning would help," Catherine put in helpfully.

"The beginning." Teddy paced. "Where is the beginning?" he muttered to himself. Then he stopped and looked directly at Isla. "Here. This orphanage. Twenty years ago. That day you and I escaped from the orphanage and wandered about the moors. After we returned, we found a carriage from London."

Isla's face remained expressionless.

She remembered that day well. Every single moment was seared into her memory.

That morning, she had been crying from hunger. There had not been enough gruel to go around, and the older children had been served first. She had been left with nothing. Jem had quietly shared his with her and then suggested they sneak out to the fields behind the orphanage. He knew where blackberries grew in the hedgerow.

She had gone with him, and sure enough, they had found the brambles and filled their bellies until they could eat no more.

"After we returned, we expected to get reprimanded. Instead, you were called into the headmistress's office, and Lady Wynthorpe was sitting there, and next to her stood Wynthorpe." He nodded at Algie. "I snuck into the connecting room and since the door was left half-open, I was able to eavesdrop."

Lady Wynthorpe and Algie had intimidated her terribly. They looked very fashionable and were clad in what looked like terribly expensive clothes. And it had been the first time for Isla to ever talk to such fine people. Lady Wynthorpe had lowered herself to her level, taken her hands in hers and exclaimed, "You look exactly like Helen!"

She had not understood what that meant. Helen, she later learned, had been her birth mother, the Countess Ellhall, who had died giving birth to her. A mother she had never known.

Her true mother had always been Vanya, for it was Vanya who had pulled her from the wreckage of a carriage accident in which her nurse had died. But Vanya had wasted away from a lingering illness. Before she'd died, she had taken Isla to an orphanage. Jem had followed, unwilling to leave her side. She must have left behind some clue to Isla's identity, though Isla never knew exactly what it was, because Lady Wynthorpe had eventually come for her. A close friend of Lady Ellhall, she had seen it as her duty to raise her dearest friend's daughter as her own.

Algie had been there with her.

And Algie had, of course, seen Jem eavesdrop from the other room.

Rather than exposing him and having him walloped for his impertinence, he'd merely regarded the boy with some curiosity and let him be.

"I followed you in the carriage," Teddy was saying now.

That, too, Isla remembered. After she had reluctantly climbed into the grand carriage and it moved, Jem had run after it, calling her name, shouting that they must meet again at the sundial. Again and again, he had repeated it.

And that had broken her heart. She had burst into tears and tried to fling herself from the carriage, but Lady Wynthorpe had held her tightly, murmuring soft words meant to soothe.

At their first stop, an inn along the road, Lady Wynthorpe turned to the innkeeper to ask for a light repast. In that moment, Isla broke free of the footman's grasp and ran.

Quick as a hare, she'd darted through them all and fled down the lane, all the way back to the crossroads. Not knowing which way to turn, she followed the scent of salt on the wind, crying, "Jem! Jem!" repeatedly as she ran.

She would have escaped, too, if it hadn't been for a

near-collision with a curricle, which pulled up short, and a particularly fast footman, who'd come racing after her.

Struggling and kicking, he'd brought her back, and she was bundled up in the carriage once more, shaking and crying. And none of Lady Wynthorpe's murmurs, protestations, or soothing words would make her stop crying.

Until she'd reached London, when Algie lifted her on his lap, dried her tears and began talking of pixies and fairies.

"With all the commotion you caused at the inn," Teddy continued, "what none of you realised was that while the footman was off chasing you, I had already caught up with the carriage. I managed to cling to the rear axle without being seen. Then, when the coach paused at the next stop and the footman was otherwise occupied, I slipped into the boot where the luggage was stowed. I was small and scrawny enough to wedge myself in behind the trunks, even with one already packed inside."

"That is not entirely correct," Algie said, lifting a finger. "You must recount the story accurately. For I realised all along that we were carrying a stowaway."

Teddy gave him a small smile. "Of course you did. And for some reason that still eludes me to this very day, you chose not to say or do anything about it, even though you knew."

Isla's mouth fell open. "Wait. Stop. Are you saying you were with us in the carriage? The entire way to London?"

Teddy tilted his head slightly. "Naturally."

"And Algie knew?"

He nodded. "I was curious to see what he would do next. I had already noticed him at the orphanage, just as he said, hiding behind the door and eavesdropping on us. While Mama was speaking to you, I wandered into the other room for a closer look. A scrawny, scraggly, half-starved thing, with a pair of dark, clever, defiant eyes. A ferocious little thing, more animal than human. He did not run when I confronted him. Said he was there to protect you. There was something about him. Something I liked. Perhaps it was the fire in his eyes or that sense of loyalty that was quite extraordinary for a boy his age. None of the London lads have that kind of steel. They are far too soft, far too spoiled. I liked that. I liked it very much. I decided to see what he would do. And I was right. He was resourceful enough to get himself to London with us. But go on. Tell us in your own words. Finish your tale."

"When the carriage pulled up in Grosvenor Square, I waited for the right moment to climb out of the boot," Teddy said. "But I waited too long. The lid opened, and he pulled me out." He shrugged and nodded towards Algie. "He made me an offer I could not refuse."

Algie retrieved his snuffbox from his waistcoat, flipped it open, and took a pinch. "Best offer I ever made."

Catherine bounced in her chair, clapping her hands. "How wonderful. What a story. I am quite breathless. Now tell us, Linwood, what was that offer?"

Teddy shrugged. "He bought me. Body and soul."

But the harshness of his words was softened by a fond smile.

Algie folded his arms. "I saw great potential in him. I needed men who possessed those characteristics. Men who are utterly loyal. Fierce. Passionate. Clever. Entirely dependent on me, of course. So, I decided to raise him for the Home Office."

"You raised him?" Isla echoed.

"Yes. He became the father I never had," Teddy said simply. "And in that one thing, his calculation was correct. My loyalty to him is absolute. I would give my life for him."

Isla drew in a sharp breath and looked at Algie with disbelief. "This entire time. All this time, I was looking for Jem. You knew where he was?"

Algie shifted uncomfortably in his chair. "Well. That's the thing." He cleared his throat. "That may be what I'll have to atone for."

"But why? Why didn't you just tell me? Why couldn't you just have...." Isla slumped in her chair, as she couldn't even bring herself to complete the sentence.

"Jem became one of the biggest secrets of the Home Office," Algie attempted to explain. "I didn't want anyone to know who he was, or what I needed him for. No one knew. No one at all. I had him set up in a separate house, with a separate staff, and he received his own special education. During the day, he trained and studied with a variety of tutors. I had to make sure the staff changed regularly. Then I had him sent off to join the army. He excelled there, too. After he returned, his training continued. By then, his father noticed and acknowledged him as being his legitimate son and heir."

Teddy nodded. "It came as a bit of a surprise because I'd always assumed I was his natural son, born out of wedlock, but that he'd never acknowledge me. But he did, shortly before he died. I suppose he was relieved his son wasn't the scum he feared he'd be, but I had grown into something useful after all. But I never had any relationship with him, not the way I had with Wynthorpe."

"By then, I had my plan crafted meticulously to the tiniest detail," Algie continued. "I needed good, reliable intelligence. Not just some common informant; I had plenty of those, but a highly trained agent, someone raised for the task. He would insert himself into the world of crime and make himself a reputation and operate from within.

"I know you missed and loved him, and it pained me to see you so sad. But my claim on him was bigger. I needed him more."

Isla turned to Teddy, a look of disbelief in her eyes. "Why did you even agree to such a mad scheme?"

"Can you truly be asking this question? The proposal was heaven sent. I was a homeless orphan. They called me a half Gypsy boy with no prospects, no education, no future. I was about to lose the only person who mattered to me. Then appeared Wynthorpe, as if sent by fate, and offered me the opportunity of a lifetime. He proposed to not only give me a home, but an education. All he wanted was my undisputed loyalty. Naturally I took it." He paused, clasping his hands behind his back. "But it came at a price." He looked at her with sorrow. "You."

"The condition was harsh: I was to remain a stranger to you. I was not to see or contact you, for that would render everything void."

"That is what I do not understand. Why? It appears to be unnecessarily cruel."

Algie rubbed his neck. "To get you to move on. To get you to focus on your new life. And to forget your old one, which included Jem. Jem needed to grow into his new identity, and to fulfil his mission he needed to be kept from all distractions. You would have kept reminding him of who he was and where he came from. It would have been an interference that could have jeopardised the entire mission."

Teddy crouched down on the floor and took her hands in his. "I saw you from afar, watched how you grew up into a beautiful young lady. Every time you and Lady Wynthorpe walked through the Whitehall Courtyards, you would see us training, and you did not know I was there. It took all the restraint I had in my being not to call out to you."

Isla was quiet as she remembered the times when she walked across the courtyard of the Horse Guards Parade towards Whitehall Palace, with her hand tucked in Lady Wynthorpe's. She remembered the group of men standing in a line for inspection, and she'd assumed they were soldiers. She had not known that Jem was amongst them. He'd been right there all the time. Under her very nose.

"But I never forgot," she whispered.

"Yes, you never forgot." Algie sighed. "It turned out to be a problem."

All the years of searching.

Why had Algie allowed it?

"You let me grieve for him. Alone. Year after year. It was cruel." Her voice shook. "And then you let me believe for months that he'd died. As a criminal."

Algie rubbed his neck. "Contrary to what the papers reported, the operation hadn't been entirely wrapped up. There were complications. Even with Night gone from the street, his enemies weren't. It took us all this time to round everyone up. I could not risk letting you know Teddy was alive—not yet. Impulsive as you are, you would have set out to seek him. It was best to wait until it was all truly brought to an end. You must forgive me, but I thought I was doing the right thing for your own protection. We completed the mission, better than we had dared hope, even. But yes. It all came at the cost of deceiving the person I care about most. Lying to you like that... it was bitter. And I do not know whether you will ever be able to forgive me for that."

In the silence of the room, only the fire crackled.

Suddenly, it all got too much. The worried expression on Catherine's face, Algie's pleading look. Teddy... Teddy...Jem... She felt an odd numbness, like an ice-cold hand squeezing her heart.

Isla got up abruptly and walked to the door.

"Isla. Where are you going?" Teddy followed her and reached out a hand towards her.

She backed away.

"I need to think," Isla said, her voice toneless.

She opened the door and addressed the maid, who was waiting there. "Have the coach made ready."

"Isla!" Teddy followed her out into the foyer with quick steps. "Are you leaving?"

"Yes."

"I'll come with you, then," Catherine offered, rising from her seat.

Isla shook her head. "No. I need to be alone. Please."

"Let her go. Let's give her some space." Algie rubbed his temple.

"If you need to be alone to think, I will respect that." Teddy searched her face. Once more, he reached out a hand and dropped it. "Take as much time as you need. I'll be waiting for you," he added softly.

Isla turned without answering and walked into the night, past the others, towards the waiting coach. The cold air stung her cheeks, but she welcomed it. It helped her feel something. Anything.

Chapter Twenty-Six

ISLA WAS TREMENDOUSLY BUSY.

When she wasn't visiting charities, the Foundling Hospital, or Newgate Prison, she helped Mrs Fry plan meetings for an organisation named 'The British Ladies' Society for Promoting the Reformation of Female Prisoners'. It wasn't quite established yet, and many meetings had to take place in the private home of Mrs Fry, or in Isla's.

Isla had left the Wynthorpe mansion in St. James's square, where she had lived with Algie, and, together with Aunt Agatha, moved into a smaller town house in Half Moon Street. Her maid, Meggie, came along, as well as Aunt Agatha's abigail, Esther. She hired a cook, a housekeeper and a coachman, and their small household was complete.

She couldn't have asked for more, she told herself, as she fell into bed night after night, exhausted from the day's activities.

No longer did she visit balls, operas, theatres and the

like. She was independent and dedicated her time solely to the good of society.

She hadn't seen Algie in months and only kept up with his activities through the papers. 'Lord Wynthorpe Addresses Parliament on Rising Concerns over Urban Crime,' she read one morning. And then, a few days later, 'Home Secretary Wynthorpe Unveils Sweeping New Measures for Public Order.' He was, clearly, the man of the hour and was lionised as a hero now as much as before.

She pulled a face and set the paper aside.

Of Teddy—of Jem—or whatever name he called himself now, she told herself she did not care a whit—there was no news at all. He'd disappeared into thin air.

That was just fine.

Positively fine.

She really couldn't be bothered to think about him at all.

Really.

Who had time when she was oh so very busy?

She blinked rapidly and pressed a finger against her nose bridge. "Confounded dust makes my eyes tear up," she remarked to herself and rang the bell for Meggie, to help her get ready for the day.

She had another meeting to organise and would be visiting Mrs Fry in Plashet House in East London. She paused before stepping into her carriage, then turned to her coachman.

"I'd like to make a stop at Kensington Gardens on the way," she told him.

He stared. "On the way, m'lady? Kensington

Gardens ain't on the way—very well, m'lady. We'll make a detour, then." Muttering under his breath something along the lines of how that small detour would turn into a day trip and that it would be an impossible feat to get her to Plashet House, which was on the other side of the city, in time for tea, he held the door open for her, and she climbed in.

Kensington Gardens was still bare in the winter. The gardens were dormant; the flowers cut back; the colours muted with the evergreen shrubs and brown grass, and a mist hovered over the muddy path leading to the pond.

There, near the Round Pond right by the path, stood a brass sundial on a stone pillar. It was a delicate, pretty sun dial.

And of course, exactly the kind of thing Teddy would have loved. Of course. Why hadn't she thought of it sooner? Jem had loved clocks, too. He'd loved to collect pocket watches. Mind you, Vanya had caught him and thrashed him for stealing them, and he'd had to promise her never to do so again. It was still difficult for her to make the connection between the two, that Jem had grown into Teddy, and that both were the same.

She traced a finger around the brass measuring device.

How many hours she'd spent here, waiting for Jem. At first, she'd come with Lady Wynthorpe. Then with her maid...but never, never once had he come.

Nor would he, today.

With a sigh, she turned to leave and to make her way back the path she'd come.

"The Thomas Thompion sun dial in Hampton Court

is older but not nearly as pretty," a voice said behind her, making her jump.

"They were commissioned in pairs for the privy gardens. This one is an imitation of the Thompion sun dials. I think it's done well enough."

Isla spun around.

She did not know where he'd come from, maybe from behind the chestnut trees, or the bushes, but there he stood, larger than life.

"It was the first and only time we'd passed through London," Teddy told her, studying the dial pensively. "They were renovating parts of the garden and relocating the sun dial. Even though I was a scrawny brat back then, I helped and earned myself a few coins. Then we moved north and at that intersection in Yorkshire, witnessed a violent carriage accident." He looked up into the distance, and a stray lock of chocolate brown hair fell into his forehead. "Vanya pulled you out of the arms of the woman, who'd been badly hurt, and she made her promise that she'd take care of you. Shortly after, she died."

Isla listened as if she was hearing the story, her own story, for the first time.

"You were a small thing, with large eyes and hair the colour of fire. You didn't speak much at all, and I believed you were mute." He uttered a sudden laugh. "Then we went to the village fair, where a group of boys bullied us. Imagine my surprise when you suddenly opened your mouth and uttered a range of swear words so violent, we were all taken aback. You wouldn't stop chattering afterwards."

Isla remembered only too well. She'd attached herself to Jem like a leech, singing, chattering, always following in his shadow, and he'd allowed it, good-naturedly.

He studied her. "And now, it appears, you're mute again."

He took her hands in his.

"Isla. Won't you look at me?" His voice was soft, coaxing.

She attempted to pull her hands away, but he tightened his grip.

"You are still angry."

That was an understatement. She was so blisteringly furious; it was a miracle she didn't combust on the spot. But beneath all that was another feeling entirely.

Sadness.

For the time lost, for the girl she used to be who'd believed him lost, who'd spent so much time and energy in finding him. For the boy he'd once been, forged, moulded and relentlessly hammered into the man he was now, by none other than her own brother.

And underneath all that, a flicker of endless relief that he wasn't dead and buried in Potter's Field. And then the devastating fear that she might lose him again.

The desire to throw herself into his arms and bawl her eyes out was overwhelming.

She swept the feeling away as resolutely as if it were cobwebs.

"You have every right to be," Teddy continued. "I would be as well if I were in your shoes. But I can't say I regret any of my decisions, Isla. That would be an untruth. If handed to me again, I would make the same choice. Algie saved me." He searched for words. "He gave me the chance for a new life, a new name. He is not only my superior, and the most brilliant man I have ever met, but also the father I never had. I owe him everything and my loyalty to him is absolute. But that doesn't mean the path I chose was easy. Not at all. Seeing you from afar, in all my various disguises. Not being able to tell you who I was. I wanted to run to you every day." He entwined his fingers in hers.

"Various disguises? You mean to say that you were not only Lucian Night but also..."

"A costermonger. A chimney sweep. A footman in a duke's household. A suspicious-looking ruffian who appeared to attack you in St Giles. We were in the middle of an operation, and I was trying to get you to leave when you tried to kill me with your umbrella. You nearly succeeded." He winced at the memory and rubbed the back of his head.

Isla blinked, confused. "But that man had a tattoo on his wrist..." Her eyes fell to Teddy's hand. He unbuttoned the cuff and pushed the sleeve up. There it was. Isla stared at it with round eyes. A smaller version of the tattoo that he wore on his back. The man she'd thought she'd killed with her umbrella...it truly had been Teddy. She reached out and traced the tattoo gently with one finger. "But you looked so different..."

"As I said, I was in disguise, undercover then, meeting one of the Mudlark Skulls men, when you crossed my path. Confound it, Isla, my heart nearly stopped when you ran into me just like that."

"I ran into you. You jumped out into my path, and I

274

had to defend myself with my umbrella. Oh! That means, of course, that you feigned it all. Stumbling and cracking your head on the stair, pretending to be dead."

He smirked. "I believe you did manage to knock me out for a moment, and I lost my senses. But it will be forevermore a mystery to me why it occurred to none of you to check my pulse before declaring me dead."

Isla sniffed. "I would never deign to touch a scoundrel from the rookery, dead or alive."

"Entirely understandable."

"This would explain why you were changing your clothes in the laundry room..." Isla muttered to herself.

Teddy leaned forward. "I did not quite catch what you just said. Do you care to repeat that?"

"Nothing...." Isla avoided his gaze, then lifted her eyes again with a frown. "But how did you manage to be in two places at once at the gambling hell? You were clearly sitting in the gaming room when I left, and you were still there when I returned."

He smirked. "Child's play. I used a door that leads to a secret passage with a shortcut, of course. Higgins had instructions to mislead you about the layout of the house, so you believed the room was farther away than it truly was. Once you were gone, I slipped back into the gaming room through the same door. It even bought me enough time to be in the middle of a new game by the time you returned."

"The things you said in there, really! Outrageous." Isla blushed as she recalled the words of his devilish 'pact'.

"It was all designed to frighten you away. Alas, I seem

to have accomplished the opposite." He took a step closer and smiled down at her, fondly. "Instead of frightening you away, you got even more persistent."

"I wish you had revealed yourself earlier."

"It was all part of Algie's plan. But it was meant to be temporary. There was another part of the agreement I did not tell you."

He paused.

"When he first offered to take me in, I consented to his terms. I said I would stay away from you and do as he required. But I insisted on one thing. That when it was over, when the work was done, he would permit me to go to you. That, in the end, he would offer no objection. That I might remain by your side."

Her eyes flashed. "Am I to be your prize, then?"

"It was never that."

He was no longer speaking English. His voice dropped, quiet and full of feeling, and he spoke in the language of their childhood. The language of the Rom.

"All I have done, every decision I made, was for you. I swore I would protect you, did I not? Even if it meant giving you up to the *gadje,* so you might live safe. So you could have the life I could never give you. Even if it meant severing all connections, vanishing from your world, and breaking every promise. It was the only way to keep you from harm."

He drew a breath.

"It was a sacrifice. But I made Algie swear on his life it would not be forever. That one day, when it was safe, my path would lead back to you. That it would end with you. And now it has. He has honoured his word."

He lifted her chin gently.

"Isla. Will you not look at me?"

But she turned her face away, her eyes still fixed on the ground.

"Can you find it in your heart to forgive me?"

She lowered her eyes and stared at the ground beneath her.

"Forgiveness isn't something that just happens," she finally mumbled.

"No, it is not. And I shan't pressure you. Take all the time you need. You can hate me and dislike me and curse me all you like for as long as you like. For the rest of your life, if you need to. I'll bear it all patiently. Only let me be with you while you do so. Let me hear it every day for the rest of our lives. We've been apart too long, and I can't bear to be separated from you anymore, not for a day, not even for a minute. Not anymore. Isla, is that muddy ground really that much more interesting than me?"

Finally, she lifted her eyes. "Yes. It is. At least the ground knows what it is and does what it's meant to. It doesn't change names, disappear, or come back from the dead. One knows what to expect. Not like some people."

He exhaled slowly, his voice low and steady. "Do you remember what I used to tell you? What I always wanted most. For both of us?"

What he wanted most.

Isla closed her eyes. The voice of the boy she used to know echoed in her memory, full of yearning and defiance. She remembered the way his eyes had burned with longing when he said it, as if the very dream of it kept him alive. It had seemed so far away then, so impossible for a child who had known only the road and the cold.

"A home," he whispered. He drew her close, his forehead nearly touching hers. "For you and me. Together."

A haven. A place no one could take from them.

Oddly enough, her new town house, lovely though it was, had never felt like home. Not even with Aunt Agatha's gentle presence beside her.

"I have dreamed of it all my life," he said softly. "A real home. I bought the grand house on the hill near the orphanage. There is a workshop, a room full of clocks. I thought that would be enough. But it wasn't. Do you know why?"

She could only shake her head.

"Because you were not in it. I walked through every room, and even though the clocks were ticking, all I heard was silence. I realised then that no house, no matter how fine, would ever feel like home without you. For someone like me, who grew up without walls or anchors, the word itself has always been elusive. But I wanted it. I wanted it with you."

He looked down, a half-smile curving his mouth. "I even filled the dining room with clocks. I found a Tompion, by-the-by, a special edition made of—"

"Oh, be quiet." Her voice trembled, but her eyes were fierce. "When are you finally going to do it?"

He blinked. "Do what?"

"You know."

He gave a faint, puzzled shake of his head. "I don't have the faintest idea what you could mean."

"Kiss me." Her fingers curled into his lapel, pulling

him down to her. "There has been far too much talking. All these words. From the moment I saw you again at the orphanage, all I've wanted is—"

He took off his spectacles, slipped them into his coat pocket, and cupped her face in his hands.

Then he kissed her. Passionately. Deeply. Reverently.

Finally.

Epilogue

THEY WERE MARRIED TWICE.

The first ceremony took place in the little chapel at Teddy's mansion in Yorkshire, with a priest and Algie and Catherine as witnesses. It was a sweet, brief ceremony, simple and to the point.

When the priest declared them man and wife, Teddy looked at Isla with such a deeply moved expression on his face, it brought tears to her eyes. He cradled her face in his hands as if she were the most precious thing he had ever held, and kissed her so lingeringly and long that the priest, after a while, cleared his throat.

"There, there," he said, "we're still here, you know."

Algie and Catherine chuckled, both embarrassed, both avoiding each other's eyes. Teddy released her, and Isla, blushing, had to reorient herself, for she had forgotten her surroundings entirely.

The second wedding took place that night.

They had come from all over Yorkshire, pulling into

281

the lawns with their carts and covered wagons, setting up camp in the surrounding lands and parks.

"You cannot be man and wife without my blessing," Lazlo said, after stepping down from his wagon. He looked at them sternly, for his word was law.

They were both clad in the traditional Romani costume: Isla wore a flowing skirt and a white blouse, and Teddy an intricately embroidered waistcoat over a linen shirt and leather trousers. Isla looked at him admiringly. He had never looked so handsome, so truly himself.

Lazlo, the leader of the Rom, married them according to the Romani ritual, which involved binding their hands with a cord. Then, everyone erupted in cheers, and the ensuing celebrations lasted several days and involved a lot of music and dancing. The entire village was involved, and there was a general sense of cheerful festivity.

"What wouldn't I give for Vanja and Mother to be here? I was lucky to have three mothers, you know? I know Mama, in particular, would have loved it," Isla said wistfully, as she watched several men build a bonfire.

"I am certain they are," Teddy replied. "Particularly Vanja. She's here with us right now."

Everyone was clapping and laughing and shouting and looking at them, and Isla glanced at Teddy with a question in her eyes.

"They want us to jump," Teddy laughed. "Over the bonfire. It's the tradition. Only then will we be truly wed in the eyes of the Rom."

"Oh, I remember," Isla exclaimed, for she had attended many a Romani wedding. Teddy looked at her. She looked at him. He extended his hand.

"Shall we, then?"

She nodded, took his hand, and together, they jumped.

SEVERAL MONTHS LATER, after the last of the wagons had departed with promises to return, and a wet spring had blossomed into a tender summer, Isla sat with Catherine on the verandah of her new home.

"To this day, I still cannot believe you truly forgave them. Just like that," Catherine said, setting down her teacup with a delicate clink. "I must possess a most unforgiving nature compared to yours. If I had been in your shoes, I would have whacked them both with my umbrella and vowed never to speak to either of them again. Scoundrels and liars, the pair of them."

They sat in the morning room of Roseview Mansion. Sunlight streamed through the French windows, which opened onto a broad verandah overlooking a sweeping park, and beyond that, the shimmering sea.

Isla nodded. "That is precisely what I did, more or less. I left and didn't speak to either of them for weeks."

Catherine narrowed her eyes. "Yes, but you didn't remain angry. That's the marvel. I remember returning weeks later and finding you and Linwood on the verandah, locked in such an embrace, I nearly dropped my parasol. I vow I have never seen a couple kiss with such fervour, and you never even noticed I was there."

"And you had brought Wynthorpe."

"Yes. I thought it was time the two of you reconciled."

Isla cleared her throat. "I had the opportunity to

wallop Algie with my umbrella shortly after we arrived here. You had stepped outside to speak with Linwood."

She had raged and wept and hollered and struck him with her umbrella, and Algie had not tried to defend himself. He had stood there like a whipped puppy and even suggested she strike his shin for good measure, which she had. Then she had dropped the umbrella and burst into tears. Then Algie had burst into tears. And they had collapsed into each other's arms, weeping.

So much for staying furious with him for the rest of her life.

"Oh." Catherine's eyes widened. "So that's why he was limping."

"Precisely."

"Well done indeed."

"As for never speaking to them again, I decided that my comfort mattered more."

"Quite right." Catherine gave a sage nod. "You married Linwood instead, ensuring he would endure a lifetime of penance. A wise choice."

Isla nodded.

"I understand his point of view," Catherine continued. "A poor boy, a pauper, who sacrificed everything so you could have a future. He did not want you to have a life on the streets, in poverty, hunted. He stayed away so you could grow up safe, respectable, and free of scandal. How terribly romantic." She placed a hand over her heart and sighed. "How the poor boy must have suffered."

"I understand it too," Isla said quietly. "The secrecy. The sacrifice. It was all part of Algie's design." Her brow furrowed. "But that doesn't mean it was right."

284

"Wynthorpe said it was all top-secret government business," Catherine offered.

Then her voice darkened. "But Wynthorpe. He was the mastermind all along. The puppet master, pulling every string. We're all just players in his game. He truly is Mephisto incarnate." Oddly enough, from her lips, it did not sound like condemnation. There was, if anything, a glint of admiration.

"Well," she added, rising with a rustle of skirts, "do remind them from time to time that forgiveness is not the same as forgetting."

"I do not forget," Isla replied. She leaned back and glanced towards the fireplace, where the two men stood engaged in a spirited argument over their next operation. A smile curved her lips. "I remind Linwood of it every day. It's part of our agreement."

"It came with a stipulation, of course," Isla said. "Now that the operation is at an end, Algie has given Teddy a new assignment."

He was to assist in establishing a division within the Home Office charged with national security. The police force was to be reorganised, and Teddy placed at its head.

"At least he no longer has to skulk about the rookery pretending to be some criminal overlord."

"So what did you make Algie promise?"

"That he would train me," Isla replied. "As one of his agents."

"And he agreed?"

"Eventually. After considerable resistance. Agents must learn any number of things. How to fire a pistol. How to go about in disguise. How to collect intelligence.

How to behave as though one's true self is a perfect stranger. It's quite an art."

Catherine gave a thoughtful nod. "That is, in fact, the most difficult part." Then she clapped a hand over her mouth.

Isla narrowed her eyes. "Catherine."

"The weather is mild today, is it not?"

"Catherine. Do not tell me he has recruited you as well. I know the entire Wynthorpe household spies for him, from the butler to the scullery maid."

Catherine's eyes shifted away.

"Since when?"

"For some time now," she admitted. Then her shoulders slumped. "I thought he was finally going to propose. And he did make a proposal, but it turned out to be for espionage."

Isla's mouth fell open. "I am shocked."

"So am I."

"I mean, I am shocked he still hasn't proposed to you."

Catherine set down her teacup carefully. "He never really did, no."

"The scoundrel."

"He gave me a ring, however," Catherine added pensively, pulling out a necklace from around her neck, on which a ring dangled.

Isla was speechless. "What? He gave you a ring?"

"Yes. After we jumped over the bonfire."

Isla sat up straight. "You jumped over the bonfire with him?"

Catherine nodded. "Shortly after you and Teddy

jumped over the bonfire, Algie came to me and said, in that gruff tone of his, 'Want to give it a go as well?'—in the least romantic way possible!"

"Algie said that?" Isla stared at her with round eyes.

Catherine nodded again. "I said, 'By all means.' Then he took my hand, and we jumped."

"Catherine."

"I suppose we're married now in the eyes of the Rom. But...he neither proposed, nor were we married in church. We still need to make it official." She beamed.

"He hasn't set a date yet?" Isla shrieked.

Catherine shrugged. "He hasn't said anything about it since."

"What I do not understand is why a woman like you thinks she must wait for him to make the first move. How much longer do you intend to wait?"

Catherine's eyes widened. "You think I should...?"

Isla gave a long-suffering sigh. She shook her head over her brother's romantic ineptitude. Then she rose and marched over to the fireplace.

The men were shouting at each other, which was nothing unusual. That always happened when, according to Teddy, Algie made unreasonable demands.

"What you are suggesting is madness. Have you any notion what that would entail in terms of manpower?" Teddy's voice had taken on the icy sharpness of Lucian Night.

"You should know by now that calculating everything to the last decimal is my particular skill," Algie retorted. "All I require of you is compliance."

"Pardon the interruption," Isla interjected smoothly, taking Teddy by the arm and pulling him away.

"Isla. We are in the midst of an important discussion," Algie objected, visibly annoyed.

"Have it later, in London, at your office. Not here. Work talk is strictly forbidden in my home."

"She is quite right," Teddy said at once.

"Besides, I have urgent need of him for a far more delicate mission." She led him out, leaving Catherine and Algie alone.

Catherine stepped toward Algie with a determined glint in her eye.

"Give them a moment," Isla murmured as she closed the door behind her.

Outside, she and Teddy strolled through the park.

"What did you discuss with Algie? Was it about your new mission?"

"Indeed," Teddy replied with a snort. "But more than that, he wants me to go into politics. I daresay he is setting his sights on becoming prime minister next. And the frightening thing is, if he tried, he would almost certainly succeed."

He laced his fingers through hers as they gazed out over the sea.

"Teddy. Promise me one thing."

"Hm?"

"That we shall always be honest with each other. Let there be no secrets, no deception between us ever again."

He nodded gravely. "That, I will promise, gladly."

Isla leaned her head against his shoulder.

"We have come far, you and I," he said at last,

drawing her close. "From two orphaned Romani children wandering the roads to all of this. It is a blessing I wake up to each day, hardly able to believe it. Do you remember what I used to promise you when we were children?"

"That you would find us a home," Isla whispered. "A real home where we would be safe, you and I, together always, and no one would ever separate us again. And you kept that promise. But do you know what?"

"What?"

"I was thinking that even if we had none of this, if we had only each other, I would be content." Her gaze drifted over the landscape. "I love this place. I truly do. But home was never a place, was it? It was always you."

He pulled her to him so fiercely she could barely breathe.

"My brave, beautiful *lelori*," he murmured against her hair. "How can I ever deserve you?"

They held each other as the sun began to set over their domain, painting the sky in shades of gold and crimson. And for the first time in their lives, they were exactly where they belonged.

∾

Afterword

This novel is set in Regency England (1811–1820), when the term 'Gypsy' was commonly used by non-Romani people to refer to the Romani community. While this term is now considered outdated and potentially offensive, it appears in the story to reflect the historical language and attitudes of the period.

The Romani characters in this novel refer to themselves as 'Rom' or 'Romani,' which are the proper terms for this ethnic group. The contrast between how outsiders label them and how they identify themselves is intentional and reflects the social dynamics of the era.

Romani people in nineteenth-century England faced widespread social prejudice and legal persecution. For centuries, laws had criminalised their nomadic way of life, and many were arrested simply for travelling, camping, or working without fixed employment. These attitudes would later be codified in legislation such as the **Vagrancy Act of 1824**, which criminalised homelessness and itinerancy, but even before that, Romani communities lived under constant scrutiny and threat of arrest.

This story aims to portray Romani culture with respect, while also acknowledging the discrimination and hardships they endured in the period. Any errors in historical detail or cultural portrayal, whether due to oversight or misinterpretation, remain entirely my responsibility.

Also by Sofi Laporte

Merry Spinsters, Charming Rogues Series

Escape into the world of Sofi Laporte's cheeky Regency romcoms, where spinsters are merry, rakes are charming, and no one is who they seem:

Lady Viola's Accidental Husband

They loathe each other on sight – until a scandalous mistake binds them in the most inconvenient way possible.

Lady Emily's Matchmaking Mishap

A scheming spinster's matchmaking plans for her sister take an unexpected twist when she finds herself entangled in a charade of love.

Miss Louisa's Final Waltz

When a proud beauty weds a humble costermonger, their worlds collide with challenges and secrets that only love can conquer.

Lady Ludmilla's Accidental Letter

A resolute spinster. An irresistible rake. One accidental letter... Can love triumph over this hopeless muddle in the middle of the London Season?

Miss Ava's Scandalous Secret

She is a shy spinster by day and a celebrated opera singer by night. He is an earl in dire need of a wife - and desperately in love with this Season's opera star.

Lady Avery and the False Butler

When a hopeless spinster enlists her butler's help to turn her life around, it leads to great trouble and a chance at love in this rollicking Regency romance.

(*more to come*)

The Viennese Waltz Series

Set against the backdrop of Vienna's 1814 elegance, diplomacy, and intrigue, this series twirls through the entwined destinies of friends, enemies, and lost lovers in charming tales of love, desire and courtship.

My Lady, Will You Dance? (Prequel)

A Lost Love. A Cold Marquess. A Fateful Christmas Country House Party...

The Forgotten Duke

When a penniless Viennese musician is told she may be an English duke's wife, a quest for lost love begins.

The Wishing Well Series

If you enjoy sweet Regency novels with witty banter and a sprinkle of mischief wrapped up in a heart-tugging happily ever after, this series is for you!

Lucy and the Duke of Secrets

A spirited young lady with a dream. A duke in disguise. A compromising situation.

Arabella and the Reluctant Duke

A runaway Duke's daughter. A dashingly handsome blacksmith. A festering secret.

Birdie and the Beastly Duke

A battle-scarred duke. A substitute bride. A dangerous secret that brings them together.

Penelope and the Wicked Duke

A princess in disguise. A charming lord. A quest for true love.

A Mistletoe Promise

When an errant earl and a feisty schoolteacher are snowed in together over Christmas, mistletoe promises happen.

Wishing Well Seminary Series

Discover a world of charm and wit in the Wishing Well Seminary Series, as the schoolmistresses of Bath's most exclusive school navigate the complexities of Regency-era romance:

Miss Hilversham and the Pesky Duke

Will our cool, collected Headmistress find love with a most vexatious duke?

Miss Robinson and the Unsuitable Baron

When Miss Ellen Robinson seeks out Baron Edmund Tewkbury in London to deliver his ward, he wheedles her into staying—as his wife.

About the Author

Sofi writes sweet, mischievous Regency romances filled with witty banter and heart-tugging happily-ever-afters. A globetrotter at heart, she was born in Vienna, grew up in Seoul, studied Comparative Literature in Maryland, and lived in Quito before settling in Europe.

When not crafting stories, Sofi enjoys exploring medieval castle ruins, taking leisurely walks with her dog, and embracing the rewarding challenge of raising three multilingual children.

Get in touch and visit Sofi at her Website, on Facebook or Instagram!

amazon.com/Sofi-Laporte/e/B07N1K8H6C

facebook.com/sofilaporteauthor

instagram.com/sofilaporteauthor

bookbub.com/profile/sofi-laporte

Made in United States
Orlando, FL
24 July 2025

63244190R00176